ALSO BY CONSTANCE LOMBARDO

Mr. Puffball: Stunt Cat to the Stars

Mr. Puffball: Stunt Cat Across America

ESCAPE
from
CASTAWAY ISLAND

HARPER
An Imprint of HarperCollins Publishers

FAME and RICHES, Here I come.

Library of Congress Control Number: 2017943582
ISBN 978-0-06-232071-1

Typography by Carla Weise
18 19 20 21 22   CG/LSCH   10 9 8 7 6 5 4 3 2 1
❖
First Edition

To my parents,
Rita and Joseph Lombardo,
for telling me
I could do anything

Baking It Big

*I*t was go time. Time to seal the deal and claim my rightful victory.

Time to bake the biggest, bestest birthday cake ever.

That's right. I was on the hit reality TV show *Celebrity Birthday Cake Wars*, where famous cats show off their mad pastry skills. And it was the seven-layer-cake round.

I know what you're thinking: Mr. Puffball, what are you doing on reality television? Your dream, as established in your first two Hollywood memoirs, is to be a movie star.

True. But let's face it. Reality television can turn an ordinary cat into a famous cat. And famous cats become movie stars. Especially if they star in movies after being discovered on a reality TV show.

So there I was, baking my heart out. I had made up the following recipe, digging deep into my culinary powers:

The Best Seven-Layer Birthday Cake EVER

Ingredients
- Lots of flour
- Even more sugar
- Rainbow sprinkles
- Over a dozen eggs
- Bucketful of butter
- A jug of heavy-ish cream
- 1 teaspoon of vanilla extract
- 3 pinches of salt
- Large bowl of anchovies

Directions
1. Melt butter with warmth. Mix together all ingredients except anchovies. Well!
2. Pour the batter into seven pans.
3. Arrange anchovies throughout, leaving aside two pawfuls.
4. Bake to perfection in a hot oven.
5. Frost cake vigorously. Use frosting to glue layers together.
6. Use remaining anchovies to spell out "Happy Birthday."
7. Eat and be happy.

And that's just the cake part! I'd love to tell you what's in Mom's Secret Recipe for Delicious Yellow Icing, but, as you may have guessed, it's a secret. Let's just say sugar and cheddar whip and yellow.

Focus, Mr. Puffball!

I wiped my brow with the side of my paw as I hunkered down for round three. In round one, I'd beaten Jennifer Pawprints as thoroughly as I'd beaten the eggs. In round two, I'd whipped Chris Purr-att as completely as I'd whipped cream.

Now it was down to me and Benedict Cumbercat. And his seven-layer Victoria sponge cake with salmon flakes was well on its way to amazing. I breathed in the salmon-y aroma. *Mmmm.*

Focus, Mr. Puffball! I forged ahead, knee-deep in flour and all those other ingredients. I combined, blended, and mixed like crazy until I was covered in a coating of powdery, sugary stuff.

And I smelled delicious.

Oh, how the studio audience cheered! They wanted me to win. I could feel their winning wishes in the very fiber of my being. Plus they kept yelling things like "You're the best!" and "USA!" and "You should totally win!"

And here's where I should mention the less-than-wonderful thing. There was a reason why, even if I, Mr. Puffball, successfully baked the world's best seven-layer birthday cake with the world's cheesiest, yellowest icing, I was not about to become famous. Can you see why?

Yes, I was on *Celebrity Birthday Cake Wars* not as myself, but disguised as my BFF, the mega movie star El Gato. Why? Because El Gato was the one who had gotten this gig, not me.

But yesterday, as I was congratulating him for his upcoming appearance on *Celebrity Birthday Cake Wars*, El Gato surprised me with a surprising question:

Shocking, I know. Of course, there was an important reason El Gato couldn't appear on *Celebrity Birthday Cake Wars*: he had to work a benefit to raise money for cats in need. Evidently, a volcano had erupted in downtown Beverly Hills, leaving many cats covered in volcanic ash and in need of a good scrubbing.

I agreed right away. If a volcano disaster had happened right in our hometown, and El Gato was helping those poor cats, even if I hadn't heard anything about a volcano, of course I'd go on *Celebrity Birthday Cake Wars* in his place.

Thus was I removing the fluffy cake layers from the steaming oven with oven mitts, dressed as El Gato. So was I ladling cheddar-y buttercream between said layers to stick them together, and icing like a maniac, disguised as El Gato. Hence was yellow-on-yellow piping generously applied, the ladder to the top of the ten-foot cake climbed, the finishing florets set in place.

And voilà!

I leapt from the ladder like a true stunt cat, did a double flip on the way down, and landed on my feet.

The three judges rushed over to Benedict. I held my breath as they stuffed their faces with his seven-layer Victoria sponge cake with salmon flakes and made yummy noises. Finally, one of the judges said, "Delicious!"

Uh-oh!

"Mmm," said another judge, licking his paws. But the third held up a dissatisfied claw. "The salmon flakes," he said drily, "are rather dry."

I let out my breath. The judges came over. "Looks wonderful, El Gato!" Three paws reached out and scooped up some anchovy birthday cake with cheddar-y frosting, followed by more happy lip-smacking.

The judges formed a brief huddle, then turned back to Benedict and me. "Both of you have made exceptional birthday cakes," said the biggest judge. "But there can only be one winner. One of you will go home with the trophy. The other will just go home."

She gestured toward a stage cat. He picked up the Golden Birthday Cake trophy and walked straight to Benedict Cumbercat. My heart sank. *Bummer.*

But wait. Just as Benedict was happily reaching out for the trophy, the stage cat veered sharply to the right and handed the trophy to *moi.*

The crowd went wild. But not for me, my friend. Not for me.

It was bittersweet. Sweet because I'd won. Sweet because I licked icing off my fur. Bitter because nobody knew it was me in that cape.

Yes, I smiled. But it was the kind of smile where your mouth goes up on one side only.

At least I knew I was in some small way helping the victims of that volcano eruption I hadn't heard about until El Gato told me about it. Surprising that I hadn't seen it on TV, but El Gato explained that the cats involved were camera shy.

Later, while waiting for the bus home and thinking about how my dreams of stardom would have to wait for another day, something caught my eye. A newspaper, lying in the street, looking as dejected as I felt.

I snatched it up. That volcano eruption was sure to be front-page news.

Perhaps it was second-page news.

FLYING SAUCER HOAX!
This photo of an airborne FRISBEE had our best UFO-enthusiasts fooled. "I thought we were about to meet our alien overlords," said one witness. "I can't believe I put on my aluminum foil cap for nothing. I...

and somebody's got a lot of explaining to do," said the duck.

FLEAS HAVE CATS FLEEING
A community of fleas, more extensive than anything this city has ever seen before, was discovered in an old abandoned warehouse just south of the city. "This is a statewide epidemic," said one official. "Sacramento is in ruins."

Why Dogs Should Not Write Advice Columns
OP-ED piece by Wilma Furguson
Dogs don't understand love. I should know; I once dated a dog. All he wanted to do was smell trees. Sad. Look, I actually like dogs. A lot. But I do not want them telling me how to live my life. If dog... write...

VOTE TODAY FOR YOUR **FAVORITE** *FLUFFY KITTEN!*
DETAILS on Page 32

No article about the volcano. Not even in the Happenings about Town section, all the way in the back. If a volcano wasn't a happening about town, nothing was.

I lowered the newspaper and stood at the bus stop on that hot, windy street, thinking and thinking. I thought about how rain in Hollywood is big news. I thought of how the snow dusting we got in Hollywood last year led to the biggest headline I'd ever seen:

And yet this volcano El Gato told me about was suspiciously absent from the news.

There were only two possible explanations:

1. The *Hollywood Times* thought a devastating volcano in downtown Hollywood was too terrible to report.
2. There was no volcano eruption, meaning El Gato had lied to me.

Which is more believable?

Sometimes it's hard to face the truth, even when it's staring you right in the furry face. But now I had to face it. El Gato was a liar. And I was the fool who trusted him.

Until now.

Good-bye, Old Friend.
Hello, Opportunity!

As I stomped over to Purramount Studios the next morning to give El Gato a piece of my mind, memories of his outrageous lies came flooding back.

And what kind of friend had I been to El Gato? Simply the best. When El Gato needed me to do a thing, I didn't make up a lie to weasel out of it (my apologies to weasels everywhere). I did the thing.

I was there for him. Even if it meant posing as him on *Celebrity Birthday Cake Wars* and getting covered in pastry flour, which was very hard to wash out!

I marched into Purramount and knocked on El Gato's door, wondering what excuse he'd give for tricking me. Maybe he'd say he was allergic to flour. Maybe he'd claim he was giving an inspiring TED Talk. Or maybe he thought a baking show was beneath him, because he was so rich and famous.

I knocked harder. No answer. He probably knew I was onto him and was hiding under the covers.

"I know you're in there," I growled. Because I could just picture him inside, peeking over his bedsheets, conjuring another lie.

"I'm coming in!" I rammed the door like the stunt cat I am, and it flew open and I fell into the room. Then I popped back up, slammed the door shut, and held forth an accusatory claw.

"You've got a lot of nerve . . . ," I started. I stopped. El Gato was not in his bed. Perhaps he was under the bed! I snuck closer and bent down to peer into the shadows. "Got you!"

He wasn't there either.

I gazed around his superstar living quarters, and my eyes stopped on the wardrobe I'd so feverishly admired in the past. Back when I was an innocent young cat, this assortment of costumes and fabulous shoes had wowed me like I'd never been wowed before.

Now all I saw were the clothes of a liar.

I tore my eyes away. Next to me was El Gato's big mirror, which he probably stared into, laughing and saying, "Ha! That Mr. Puffball believes everything I say. What a dope!" On the table was today's newspaper, which El Gato had probably read this very morning with those lying eyes while . . .

Wait a minute. What's this? I leaned closer.

..which was a Hollywood shocker the likes of which this reporter has never seen.
— GINGER TABBY STAFF WRITER

WINNING ENTRY IN "WORLD'S FLUFFIEST KITTEN" CONTEST.

YOU

THE MYSTERIOUS R

• Are you totally **AWESOME?**
• Do you long for **FAME+FORTUNE?**
• Could you beat the **FELINE NINJA WARRIOR CHAMPION?**

IF SO, come AUDITION FOR **FELINE NINJA WARRIOR** NEXT Saturday at REALITY STUDIOS, 10 ELM St., HOLLYWOOD, CA (NEXT to the SHRIMP 'R' US)

Feline Ninja Warrior! Seriously? Was El Gato thinking of going on my favorite reality TV show? Or would he try and trick me into going on dressed as him again?

Let me tell you something about reality TV shows. Many of them are staged. Fake. Full of phony baloney.

My friends had been on reality TV shows, and they told me all about it.

Whiskers on *Prancing with the Stars*

Kitty on *Oldsters Got Singing*

Pickles on *Kitten Swap*

Chet on *Checkers with the Elderly Stars*

But *Feline Ninja Warrior*, the most popular reality TV show in my house and many other houses, was different. No tricks. No gimmicks. No makeup. Just the toughest of the tough, proving their toughness through tests of agility, strength, and general manliness.

A *Feline Ninja Warrior* championship meant stardom, and money, and respect. And here was my chance to get all those things. With a little extra training with my friend Bruiser, I could win that championship easy-peasy.

And I wouldn't do it dressed as El Gato. No, the only costume I'd wear to become the next *Feline Ninja Warrior* champion was my signature classic bow tie.

Click!

Somebody was turning the door handle. In a moment, El Gato would be inside. The last time this happened, all the way back in my first book, I'd hidden in fear. But there was nothing to fear anymore. I'd come to give El Gato a piece of my mind, and that's what I was going to do.

I stood with my legs planted firmly. One paw held the newspaper with the *Feline Ninja Warrior* ad, and the other rested saucily on my hip.

El Gato stepped into the room and spotted me right away.

"Mr. Puffball," he said, not unpleasantly, "I'm glad you're here. It looks like you found the ad I wanted to show you . . ."

"Oh, no you didn't!" I countered, waving one finger back and forth. "You're not going to lie to me again . . ."

"About that . . . ," he started, but I interrupted with a louder voice.

"So you admit it! Well, I'm done listening to your lies. I am going to audition for *Feline Ninja Warrior* dressed like myself, acting like myself, and smelling like myself!"

"My idea exac—"

"I'm not interested in your idea! No amount of begging or trickery could make me go on that show as you. I am Mr. Puffball, I don't need you anymore, and I am never speaking to you again!"

I crossed the room, grabbed the door handle, looked over my shoulder, and said, "By the way, your costume collection is tacky!"

With that, I stormed out.

"Now I'm not talking to you either!" yelled El Gato as I stomped down the hall.

"Good!" I yelled louder.

"Works for me!" yelled El Gato even louder.

Good-bye, BFF who always gets me into trouble. Good-bye, buddy who is much more famous than me. Good-bye, liar who forced me to bake the world's most delicious cake and not get any credit for it. Or even taste it.

I quickly arrived at the place where the new Mr. Puffball would be born. A new Mr. Puffball who didn't need rich, famous, lying friends. A Mr. Puffball who was about to become a rich and famous reality TV show champion on his own terms.

A Whole New Puffball

Bruiser is a very big cat with an even bigger heart. And even bigger biceps.

He was my trainer when I first came to Hollywood and became a stunt cat to the stars. Back when I thought El Gato was the coolest cat in the world—just because he was a Hollywood superstar with a supercool limo.

A familiar voice broke through these painful memories. "Puffyball," said Bruiser. "Why you come here?"

"Because of this," I said, handing him the *Feline Ninja Warrior* ad.

Bruiser studied the ad. Then he looked me over. "To beat the Mysterious R is very challenges."

"Yes, but with your most intense training . . ."

"Could be happen, yes," finished Bruiser. "You must work so much your head maybe explode. Every day, all the day, muscle building, balance making, speed walking, and of course paw-to-paw combats. Is what you want?"

Sometimes Bruiser doesn't know his own strength.

I stood and stuck out my chest. "Let's do this thing!"

As we walked into the cavernous building filled with scary equipment, I recalled our early days together. Bruiser trained me hard that first time, with rocky mountain climbing, cruel horseback riding, and enormous weight lifting.

But now that he had his own school, Bruiser had taken it up a notch.

Weight Lifting Chin-Ups

Extreme Balance Yoga

Total Combat Fitness

At times it hurt so bad in so many parts of my body, my brain begged me to give up. But I shushed my brain and powered on. With fame beckoning like light at the end of a pain-filled tunnel, I could bear anything.

Except Bruiser's irritating new assistant.

Yes, Pickles the kitten was working with Bruiser as part of his own dream—to become a Hollywood stunt cat. He had the chops to be a stunt cat. The problem was, he was so adorable, nobody took him seriously.

Every night, I went home to my oldster friends who were always there for me with an uplifting song, nourishing grub, and a jumbo-size box of Band-Aids.

And Pickles the kitten, who lived with us too. *Ugh.*

The only cat missing was Rosie. She'd recently sent a postcard saying she was off on a trip and would be gone for a while. (Of course, El Gato was also missing, but that was because we were now enemies, not even frenemies.)

And then one day, when I arrived at Bruiser's

school for my final day of training, there stood Rosie.
Looking as cute as ever.

Oh! I blushed under my fur. I blushed with the knowledge that Rosie had those special feelings neither of us had ever spoken aloud.

Because of her special feelings, she hated the thought of me getting hurt on *Feline Ninja Warrior*. How it would pain her to see me climbing the Wall of Hot Spikes, or balancing atop the slender Wobbly Board, or getting pummeled in the Ultimate Kung Fu Challenge.

"It's okay . . ." I started, but she'd already walked away.

But a smile bloomed across my face anyway. For now I knew my dear Rosie would be in the television audience, her eyes glued to my every move, worrying over every danger, cheering at every triumph. Crying, maybe, because she was so proud of her handsome Mr. Puffball.

Ironically, her request that I not go on the show strengthened my resolve. Knowledge of her special feelings was exactly the advantage I needed to beat the Mysterious R.

The Mysterious R . . .

The Mysterious R . . .

Pickles woke me from my reverie.

I looked down into his oversize eyeballs and nodded like a macho cat. "Bring me my kangaroo boxing gloves, please."

Even though that day was the hardest day in a week filled with hard days, I didn't mind.

I'd faced physical challenges beyond the threshold of feline endurance and been transformed into a formidable foe, ready to take on the Mysterious R. And become the new Feline Ninja Warrior.

Those were the words I repeated throughout the next day during my strenuous *Feline Ninja Warrior* audition. And guess what?

I aced it.

I left the audition, ready to skip all the way home, or maybe take the bus since my legs were tired, when I found myself surrounded by a group of journalists.

"Yes," I told those reporters, sticking out my now-muscular chest, "I do have something to say."

Feline Ninja Warrior

"**B**efore you go out there to compete," the producer said to me and the Mysterious R the next day, "know that this show is not like other reality TV shows. Our Wall of Hot Spikes is really hot. The Wobbly Board actually wobbles. And we expect you to hold nothing back during the Ultimate Kung Fu Challenge."

"That's right," said one of the camera crew. "You know the saying 'safety first'?"

The Mysterious R and I glanced at each other and nodded.

"Well, we don't say that here," said the producer. "You go out there, shake paws, and then let loose the cats of war. Winner takes all. Loser takes all kinds of hurting."

I took a deep breath. The Mysterious R looked like he wanted to say something, but didn't. Then we strode out together, under the glare of bright lights and a sea of cheering cats. Some yelled, "Mysterious R rules!" Others yelled, "Go, Mr. Puffball, go!"

We arrived at the starting square, where we'd begin our race to fame and fortune.

But first, the paw shake. I looked into the eyes of the Mysterious R, hidden behind a face-covering mask. I thought I saw a familiar sparkle there, almost like . . .

Focus, Mr. Puffball!

We assumed our places, our bodies tensed with anticipation, our fur slicked aerodynamically down, tails streamline straight. The starting bell rang out—

CLANG!

And we were off on a series of death-defying challenges that went something like this:

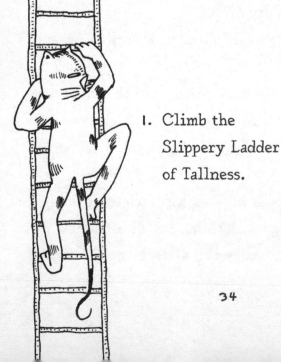

1. Climb the Slippery Ladder of Tallness.

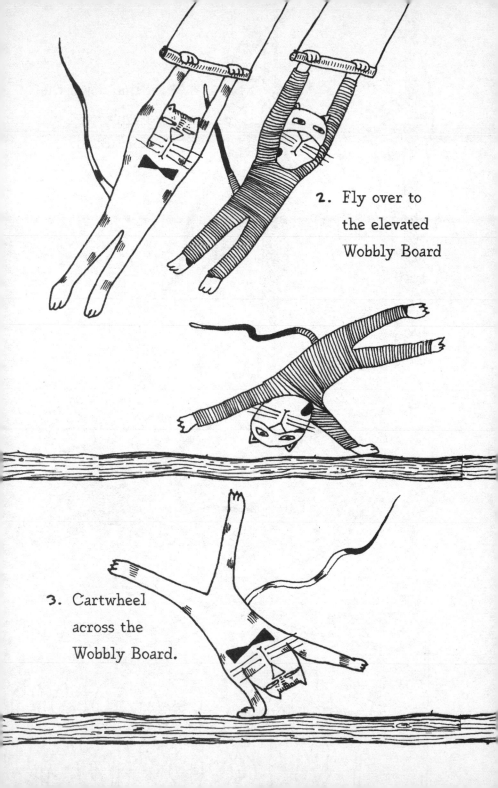

2. Fly over to the elevated Wobbly Board

3. Cartwheel across the Wobbly Board.

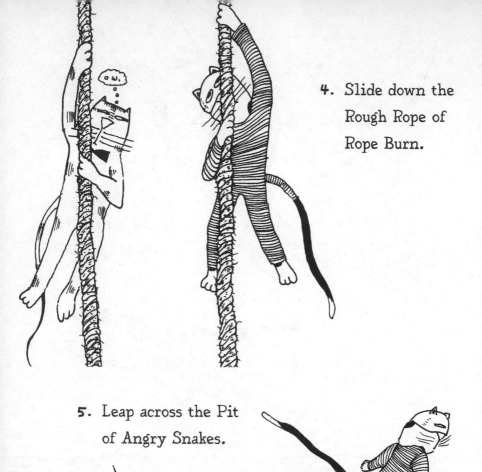

4. Slide down the Rough Rope of Rope Burn.

5. Leap across the Pit of Angry Snakes.

6. Ascend the
Wall of
Hot Spikes.

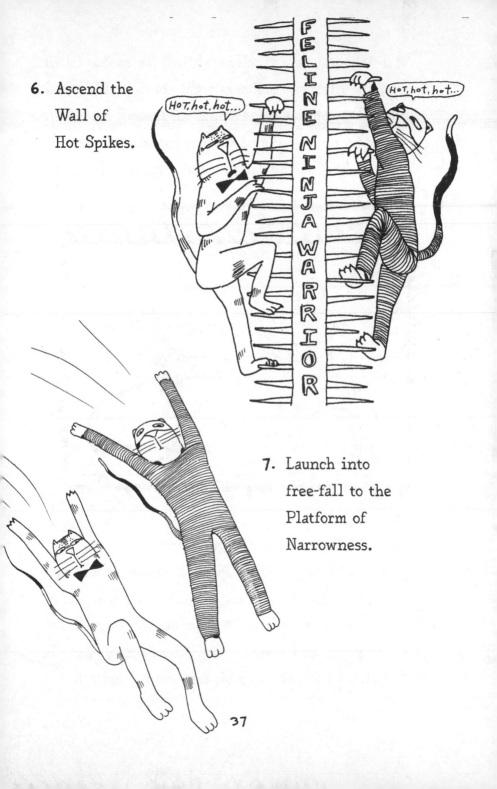

7. Launch into
free-fall to the
Platform of
Narrowness.

All along the muscle-straining, suspense-filled course, the Mysterious R was right there beside me. I could hear my opponent breathing hard, smell his sweat, and see him matching my awesomeness step for step.

We arrived at the finale: the Ultimate Kung Fu Challenge.

Hi-yah! Power kick! Fists of fury!

It was a fierce battle indeed. Sweat poured down my face, continued down my neck, and dampened my bow tie. The Mysterious R was super-fast. One brutal flash of paws, and I was down. The count began. It looked like I was the day's biggest loser after all.

Then I remembered Rosie. Sitting at home, whispering something like, "Don't be a wimp, Mr. Puffball."

That was all I needed. I leapt up and delivered a kick like the world had never seen before, and the Mysterious R was down. The referee counted off . . . five, four, three, two . . . ONE!

I was the winner!

And the crowd went wild. The announcer said, "We have a new *Feline Ninja Warrior* champion. And his name is Mr. Puffball!" A staff cat ran over and handed me a giant check for one million dollars.

That's right. I was rich.

Television cameras were everywhere. I was famous.

FelineNinjaWarrior   Date: 04/24/2018

Pay to the order of: *Mr. Puffball* $1,000,000.00

One Million °⁰/₁₀₀ *Dollars*

For *Awesomeness*   *Shadow Boxer*
                        AUTHORIZED SIGNATURE

"And now," continued the announcer, "we must ask the former champion, the Mysterious R, to relinquish the *Feline Ninja Warrior* champion medallion."

The Mysterious R placed the medallion over my head. I wondered who was behind that mask. Was it one of my rival stunt cats? Victory McTabby, perhaps? Rollin' Thunder? Ragnar?

I had to know. One of my paws extended to shake paws like a good sport, the other reached up and yanked the mask off the Mysterious R. And that's when I got the biggest shock ever.

I was rich. I was famous.

And I had just bummed out my best friend.

The Joys of Stardom

In the weeks that followed, I was so busy enjoying my fame and fortune, I didn't have time for one of those heart-to-heart conversations with Rosie that she-cats like so much. I did, however, send a bunch of flowers with a thoughtful note:

I'd wanted to clear things up between us on the night of my victory. I ducked into the dressing room to change out of my warrior bow tie and into my celebrity bow tie. But when I emerged, looking for Rosie among my gigantic crowd of fans, she was nowhere to be seen.

Then came a whirlwind of star-worthy activities. First there were the TV appearances. Everybody wanted to know about the real Mr. Puffball.

Next were the magazine articles, complete with photo shoots that brought out all my best sides.

And the merchandise. My goodness, the merch
was awesome.

Best of all, everywhere I went, cats of every stripe recognized me and begged me for my autograph. All day long I heard, "Mr. Puffball, sign my autograph book!" "Mr. Puffball, sign my napkin!" "Mr. Puffball, sign my tail!"

All this me-time left no room for old-friend-time.

If they wanted to see Mr. Puffball, superstar, they'd have to call my secretary, just like everybody else.

Also, all the money I'd won helped me make a life-changing realization: I needed to buy stuff. The list of expensive stuff I needed was so important, I decided to write it out as a list. I called it:

EXPENSIVE STUFF I NEED

1. A huge neon sign for the old MGM Studios, with the words "Home of Feline Ninja Warrior Champion Mr. Puffball" in blinking lights

2. An extensive new bow tie collection, including ones made of raw silk, fine velvet, and free-range cashmere. And one that had been worn by Leonardo diCatprio in *The Great Catsby.*

3. A hand-carved, solid oak bow tie closet
4. A floor-to-ceiling fridge stuffed with daily deliveries of 100 percent organic milk, all the anchovy pizza I could eat, white truffle oil yogurt mouse tails, etc.
5. One giant gold star to hang on my bedroom door

6. A life-size portrait of *moi*, painted by a world-famous artist

7. A platinum watch that told the date, the temperature, and the number of fans in the vicinity

8. And, of course, a gold limo. Not gold-painted. Not gold-plated. It was a limo made entirely of gold.

MR. PUFFBALL'S RIDE

Pickles begged me for a ride, but gold limos are not for kittens. Kitty, Chet, and Whiskers also wanted rides, but do you have any idea how much elderly cats shed? Even Bruiser asked me to help him pick up some gym equipment, but my limo was not a service vehicle!

There was one cat I did want in my limo: the adorable Rosie. So after I hired a driver strong enough to turn the wheel, I went to visit her. She'd forget she was ever mad at me for stealing her *Feline Ninja Warrior* championship once she sat in my limo and had a glass of gold-speckled, ice-cold sparkling water.

Her front door swung open, and my heart skipped a beat.

Focus, Mr. Puffball!

I shook off that weak-in-the-knees feeling and stuck out my vintage silk bow tie. "Why, hello there," I said in my most manly voice. "Long time no see, Rosie."

"Not since *Feline Ninja Warrior,*" she said, crossing her paws across her chest.

I laughed heartily. "Ha ha. What's a little kung fu fight between friends?"

The sun hit my limo, and Rosie held up her paw against the blinding glare. Then she reached out, pulled me into her home, and assumed the kung fu stance.

"I'm game," I said, readying myself for another match.

I stood and dusted the humiliation off my fur. So far, the visit was not going as I'd hoped. "Too bad you didn't do that the night of the show."

"I want to be honest with you, Mr. Puffball," she said, slumping onto the couch. I sat down next to her. "The producers told me to throw the game. They said a cat who wouldn't take off her mask could never be famous. But I wasn't after fame. You were. They insisted I let you win, or they'd find a way to disqualify us both."

I shook my head, shocked at what I was hearing. "It can't be. . . ."

"If it had been anybody else, I wouldn't have done it. I hate dishonesty. I hated throwing the game.

That's why I asked you not to be on the show."

She let me win? Impossible. I was a star ninja!

"I'm sorry to say this," I said, "but I don't believe you."

"When have you ever beaten me in a kung fu match?"

I thought back to the many times we'd sparred. I'd never beaten her at kung fu. Never. But if she'd thrown the game, what did my stardom mean?

I stood abruptly. "I have to go. Somebody somewhere wants my autograph."

Rosie looked past me, out the window, to where my limo was sparkling in the sun. "You know how I was going to spend my money, if I'd won?"

"On a life-size portrait of yourself?" I asked. "All the best stars are doing it."

She strode over to her front door and opened it. "I wanted that money to write, produce, and direct my dream project. About the life of a humble stunt cat. One who had lots of talent and even more heart. Without that money, my dream is over. Even worse, it looks like that humble stunt cat doesn't exist anymore."

I moved to the doorway and gave her my best superstar look. "I'm sorry things didn't work out for you. But I'm here to offer something even better: a ride around town in my solid gold limo. Let's dazzle the nobodies."

"I can't," said Rosie. "Because I am a nobody."

With that, she slammed the door, before I could explain that any friend of mine couldn't possibly be a nobody.

I sank into my gold velvet seat and told my driver to drive, just drive, anywhere would do. While deep in thought, a call came in on the limo video phone. It was Victoria Bossypaws, commander in chief of Purramount Studios.

Sidekick? I hadn't made my way across the country from my small town of New Jersey, befriended and then alienated El Gato, trained with Bruiser, and won the *Feline Ninja Warrior* championship to become a sidekick.

"Call me back when you're looking for a star," I said. "Because I'm Mr. Puffball. And I am a star."

I hung up just as my driver pulled into a gas station. "The tank is empty again, sir. I'll need some money to fill it up."

"Certainly, my good cat," I said, whipping out my diamond-studded wallet. I opened it. And discovered something truly horrible.

One million dollars. All gone but one. And I'd just turned down a chance to costar with Chris Purr-att in a blockbuster movie.

The Agony of
Rock Bottom

As my driver walked away from my grounded gold limo, muttering something about going back to law school, I considered my options.

1. Call Victoria Bossypaws back and beg to be in that movie.
2. Sell a million autographs for one dollar each or one autograph with really good penmanship and possibly a doodle for one million dollars.
3. Go back to being a stunt cat.

Never! I would never go back to being a stunt cat. I had moved on to bigger and better things, like reality TV, cashmere bow ties, and gold limos.

I called Victoria Bossypaws.

I almost sank into despair, right there in the back-seat of my gasless limo.

Focus, Mr. Puffball! You're too good to give up. I still had option number two.

Time to sell some autographs. I abandoned my gold limo until I could raise enough money for gas, and walked the long quarter mile to a park in downtown Hollywood. Along the way a pebble got lodged between my toes.

Could this day get any worse?

I plucked it out, found the park, and settled onto a bench. Then I carefully crafted a handmade sign and waited.

A large group of cats soon spotted me. They pointed and waved and surged my way. *Success!*

"Hello, fans!" I called as I whipped out my gold signing pen.

The cats made a sharp left turn. My eyes followed and saw who was on a nearby bench, stealing my limelight.

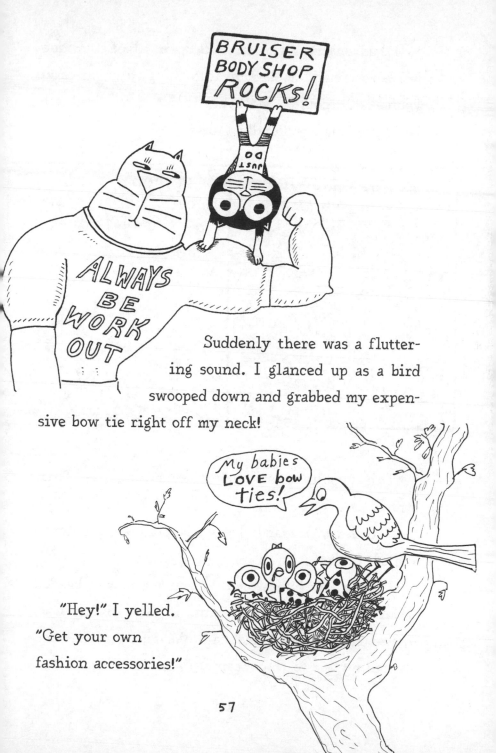

Suddenly there was a fluttering sound. I glanced up as a bird swooped down and grabbed my expensive bow tie right off my neck!

My babies LOVE bow ties!

"Hey!" I yelled. "Get your own fashion accessories!"

57

I had nearly given in to despair when a shadow fell across me. I looked up into the face of an eager young cat. I could almost feel that one hundred dollars fattening my slender wallet.

This insult to my superstardom was the final straw.

"Good day, madam!" I said, leaping up and storming out of the park.

Only a fancy feast could cheer me now. I headed toward my favorite restaurant, Pacific Dining Cat. Then I remembered the lone dollar in my wallet and steered myself to the cheapest diner in town:

The smell of anchovies frying in recycled oil hit my nostrils like a slap in the nose. I sat in a shabby booth in the back. As soon as my butt touched the seat, I felt something unpleasant. The duct tape covering a hole was peeling up and sticking to my fur. I shifted over and studied the menu.

What could I buy with just one lonely dollar?

"One kitten-size milk and a day-old cracker," I ordered. Behind the waitress, somebody swooshed past.

I glanced up and just caught sight of a fez and well-groomed stripes. El Gato! Without noticing me, he plopped down in the booth behind me.

59

I heard the crinkly snap of a newspaper being opened and an unhappy groan. I peeked over my shoulder.

I opened my mouth, then remembered we weren't speaking. And yet I longed to talk to my old friend.

We *could* talk . . . as long as he didn't turn around.

I disguised my voice by lowering it an octave and said, "What's the problem, bub?"

"Hollywood has forgotten me," said El Gato. "I was

a big star—one of the biggest. But lately, the studios aren't calling. The directors don't want me. Nobody even asks for my autograph anymore."

"Hollywood is the worst," I said.

"This town chews us up and spits us out like chewing gum," said El Gato.

"And then we find ourselves on the bottom of somebody's shoe." I sighed. A big one. "I was rich and famous for a few weeks. Now it looks like my career is over before it really began."

"Have you been in anything I might have seen?" he asked.

"Maybe," I muttered. Should I tell him who I was? First I wanted some answers. "And what have I seen you in? Any reality shows?"

"I was on *Celebrity Birthday Cake Wars. . . .*"

"Were you really?" I asked, feeling the old resentment bubbling up.

More crinkling as El Gato put down the newspaper. "No," he admitted. "I wasn't really. I had something else to do, so I tricked my best friend into going on in my place."

"Like an old piece of chewing gum," I said. "That was rude. Very rude."

I heard El Gato's cape rustling as he shifted side-ways to peer at me. The jig was up. "I know it was rude, Mr. Puffball, but . . ."

"No buts!" I ripped my fur free of the duct tape, all ready to stand and deliver a speech, but somebody showed up to ruin the moment.

"Is this one of those fake and phony reality shows?" I asked.

"Oh, no," said Brock Showman. "The *Castaway Island* experience is very real."

The *Celebrity Birthday Cake Wars* incident flashed through my brain.

"Sounds awesome!" I said. "Except one of us thinks he's too good for reality TV."

"Are you too good for two million dollars?" asked the TV producer.

El Gato and I locked eyes. His wallet sat on the table, looking almost as slender as mine.

"Will there be food on the island?" asked El Gato.

The producer laughed. It sounded like an evil laugh, but I chose to ignore it and focus instead on the two million dollars. "Of course there will be food! Enough for you and all of your friends!"

"Plenty of sunshine too, I bet," I said.

"Picture this," said Brock Showman. "Two weeks on a lush, tropical island, filled with beautiful flowers and tasty coconuts, surrounded by the endless blue sea. Hear the lapping sound of waves rolling in to shore as you and your friends compete—more like play games, really—in a competition to see who will win two million dollars."

"And eat the most shrimp," said El Gato.

"Here's your chance," said the producer, "to win back your fans and maybe win two million smackers. We want this show to focus on friendship—so we'd like you to invite your friends. You do have friends, don't you?"

My brain remembered all the times I'd refused to wash the dishes or let my friends ride in my limo. But they'd love me again if I let them appear along-side me in an island paradise reality show where we got to play games, eat coconuts, and listen to the surf!

El Gato and I jumped up at the same time.

The Whole Gang

Seven is a magical number. Seven days of the week. Seven Hairy Pawter books. The seven stripes of Seven Stripes (a cat who lives in the neighborhood).

It was also the number of cats they needed for *Celebrity Castaway Island*. Fortunately I knew seven cats who would be up for the adventure:

1. Moi
2. El Gato
3. Rosie (aka the Mysterious R)
4. Chet (movie director)
5. Whiskers (dancer)
6. Kitty (singer)
7. Bruiser (Hollywood trainer extraordinaire)
7½. Pickles (Pesky Kitten)

True, Pickles only had a bit part in *Mac & Cheesy's Excellent Adventure*. But being an adorable kitten was its own kind of celebrity. Plus Brock Showman had seen Pickles in some stupid video and insisted he come along.

Now El Gato and I had to convince our friends that they wanted to be on *Celebrity Castaway Island*.

First we looked over the list of rules the producer had given us.

CELEBRITY CASTAWAY ISLAND RULES
BY BROCK SHOWMAN

1. NO OUTSIDE FOOD.
2. DON'T PROVOKE THE WILD MONKEYS. THEY BITE.
3. ONE SMALL TRAVEL BAG ONLY.
4. NO SWIMSUITS.
5. EACH CAT MUST COMPETE IN THE *FEATS OF STRENGTH, DEEDS OF DARING. ETC.*
6. THE JUNGLE IS YOUR LITTER BOX. CHOOSE YOUR SPOT WISELY.
7. EVERY FOUR DAYS, ONE OR TWO CATS GET VOTED OFF THE ISLAND DURING *TRIBAL COUNCILS.*
8. ALWAYS OBEY BROCK SHOWMAN!
9. THE WINNING CAT WILL RECEIVE: *TWO MILLION DOLLARS.*
10. DO NOT PEE IN THE RESERVOIR.

True, some of my friends (Chet, Whiskers, Kitty) were elderly and could not handle the Feats of Strength. And Bruiser had an unfair advantage as the strongest cat in Hollywood and possibly the world.

Pickles's extreme cuteness might work against me. And I was a little nervous about the monkeys. Yes, Hollywood monkeys were all right. But monkeys in the wild had a reputation for being, well, pretty wild.

No matter what, one of us was going to win two million dollars (probably me) and that was enough money to share! (Half for me, half for everybody else.)

What's more important than money?

Before El Gato and I made it to the front door of the old MGM Studios, I was met with an unpleasant surprise.

As I lay on the ground with Pickles on my chest, Bruiser towered over me.

"Puffyball," he said, wagging one giant finger back and forth, "you get riches on ninja show. Why never give me money or say who train you: me, Bruiser!"

"Or at least donate something to our tough cat training shop!" added Pickles.

"But I did donate something. Something very beautiful."

"Give me something I can use," said Pickles.

"Follow me," I said, "and you'll get all the tough-guy equipment money can buy."

Inside, we gathered everybody together. Fortunately, Rosie was visiting Chet for their weekly How to be a Great Director workshop, so she was there too.

Time for our big announcement:

All that bad cat-titude made me fall off my stool!

Hmm...

"As the biggest celebrity here," said El Gato, "I have some great news: we're all going on *Celebrity Castaway Island*. Here's the list of rules."

He quickly flashed the list at them.

I stood and dusted myself off.

TOO MUCH REALITY-V NO GOOD!

BOD IS ME.

"The important thing is, no bathing suits, compete in some easy-peasy contests, eat lots of coconuts, soak up the sun, avoid the resident monkeys, and we get two million dollars."

COCONUTS GIVE ME gas!

BEACHES HAVE TOO MUCH SAND!

Rosie crossed her paws over her chest. "WE get two million dollars EACH?"

"Not exactly," I said. "More like, one of us gets two million dollars, and I promise I'll share it with the rest of you."

Everybody started talking at once. Their first reactions were kind of negative.

I WILL NOT WEAR A HULA SKIRT AGAIN!

WILL there be SPIDERS?

I'D ♥ RATHER BE DANCIN'

71

But then Rosie said:

And El Gato said:

And then everybody was on board!

"By the way, Mr. Puffball," asked Rosie, "have you ever seen *Celebrity Castaway Island?*"

"Not yet," I said. "But I will watch it very soon."

Rosie smiled the kind of smile that meant she had a plan. I just hoped it wasn't a plan for revenge.

Bon Voyage

Imagine the luxury cruise liner that would transport such a spectacular group of celebrities to our tropical island destination. Picture an ocean voyage complete with round-the-clock entertainment, live music, loads of comfy deck chairs, and enough shrimp to choke a horse.

And now take a gander at the old sea bucket that carried us to the island.

AHOY MATEYS!

Fortunately, El Gato had stashed a jumbo bag of yogurt-covered mouse tails in his cape, which escaped the notice of *Celebrity Castaway Island* producer Brock Showman and his crew.

Unfortunately, El Gato is not good at sharing.

The worst part of our ocean voyage was not having any milk on board. Brock said chubby cats are not winners. So he only gave us fat-free protein bars and water. I don't like water. It tastes like nothing. Or like whatever the inside of my mouth tastes like, which is sometimes not very pleasant.

DOES anyone else smell SCURVY?

Also I learned that seasickness involves a lot of throwing up. Sometimes the sound of everybody puking over the side of the ship was louder than the roar of the engine. Plus I got a splinter. Twice.

And then there was Pickles.

Don't step on that POOP DECK!

At odd times, Brock gathered us on deck for strange announcements.

Fortunately, Bruiser secretly dove off the deck twice a day to get us all the seafood we could eat. I appreciated it a lot.

And yet his extreme strength had me worried. How could I compete with that level of dude?

I needed an ally.

I realized then that my best allies would be the ones who had helped me when I first arrived in Hollywood. But when I found them:

I realized I needed a new strategy. Four days into our trip, while we were enjoying the day's Bruiser catch, I said, "It's wonderful to be here with all my friends, on our way to an exciting island adventure. Only one of us can win, yet all will benefit. Because, unlike some of us, I'm good at sharing."

Rosie glared at me with an arched eyebrow. "Says the guy who doesn't listen to his friends."

"And who buys a solid-gold limo when what we really need is a new vacuum cleaner," said Chet.

"And who forgot my birthday," added Pickles.

"When was your birthday?" I asked.

"In two months," said Pickles. "Does that jog your memory?"

"C'mon, cats," I said, desperate to win back everybody's affections before we landed on our reality TV show. "Remember in *Titanicat*, when the handsome cat is the star?"

BOOM! The ship jerked to a stop.

WHOA!!

I went skidding into the railing and was nearly thrown overboard. I clung on, peered down to the sea, and saw some friendly faces.

"Okay, celebrities," said Brock Showman, emerging from the captain's quarters. "Remember when I said challenges can happen at any time?"

"Nope," said Rosie.

"Well, I said it. And now is one of those times. It's your first Feat of Strength! Each of you must grab a rope, tie it to the railing, shimmy down, and swing into one of the waiting lifeboats. Extra points if you knock one of your friends into the water."

I wondered who I should knock into the water first. Then I remembered the true meaning of friendship and how I needed everybody not to hate me. I raised one fist. "We are not those kinds of cats! If anything, we will each lend a paw and help. . . ."

I heard movement behind me and turned to see everybody scrambling like mad toward the railing. Looked like they'd forgotten all about Team Bruiser and Team Old.

I rushed for one of the ropes and quickly tied it using a nautical knot I'd read about in the pamphlet "Nautical Knots and You." Then I slid down, only to see there was

but one lifeboat left, and it was heavily patched.

I kicked off from the ship, swung hard, and leapt into the sad little lifeboat. I located the small plastic oars and tossed my gaze across the waves to our destination—Castaway Island, many leagues away (if I understand how long a league is).

Have you ever heard the phrase *tropical paradise*?

Well, with the wide expanse of sand, dense palm-tree jungle, and distant mountains, the island certainly looked tropical. The monkey chatter and bird calls made it sound tropical. But would it be paradise?

My recent training had paid off; my biceps rippled impressively and rowed me quickly along. Still, as the last one to disembark the ship, I was way behind my so-called friends, who were eagerly rowing toward the island we'd inhabit for the next few weeks.

Of course, Bruiser was in the lead, followed by Rosie, Pickles, El Gato, and Kitty. Then I saw Chet and Whiskers:

Yes, I could row past them, pretend I hadn't noticed their elderly struggles, and land on the beach with my bicep sweat gleaming in the sun.

Or I could do a heroic deed that would make everybody like me again.

I grabbed some rope, tied it to their boats, and rowed as hard as I could. The aromatic breeze, infused with the scent of exotic flowers and overripe bananas, blew my fur askew as I powered through the waves.

All my friends were standing on the beach, watching as I gave it a final heave-ho and pulled us all in. Now they'd see what a good guy I was.

Brock Showman was there too, lit up by the late-afternoon sun, eyes narrowed. He looked less than impressed by my helpful attitude.

And so began my triumphant return to reality TV.

Welcome to Castaway Island

If you're like me, and I'm guessing you are, you enjoy a good map.

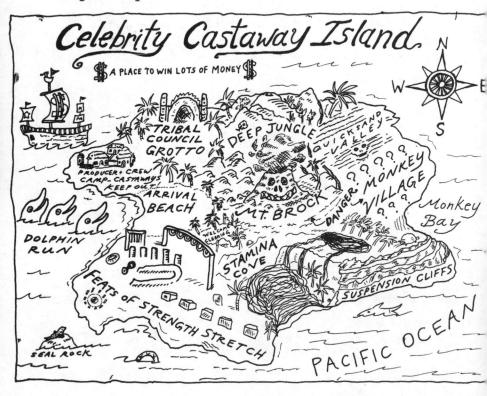

Celebrity Castaway Island

$ A PLACE TO WIN LOTS OF MONEY $

N W E S

TRIBAL COUNCIL GROTTO

DEEP JUNGLE

QUICKSAND VALLEY

PRODUCER + CREW CAMP - CASTAWAYS KEEP OUT

ARRIVAL BEACH

DANGER MONKEY VILLAGE

Monkey Bay

MT. BROCK

DOLPHIN RUN

STAMINA COVE

SUSPENSION CLIFFS

FEATS OF STRENGTH STRETCH

SEAL ROCK

PACIFIC OCEAN

This was the first thing Brock Showman handed each of us once we'd settled onto logs in the Welcome Clearing. It smelled like rotting fruit and was encircled by towering torches that cast long, scary shadows, and the logs were splintery. All in all, it was not very welcoming.

Camera cats surrounded us, filming our every ear twitch, whisker flick, and tail tremor. I determined then and there to keep my game face on at all times. No matter the grueling ordeal, extreme weather conditions, or disappointing meal, I'd look tough.

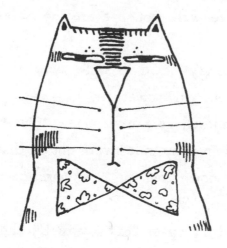

"Castaways," said Brock Showman, "I will now explain the rules of the island."

I raised my hand like a good castaway.

"If you have a question, just yell it out," said Brock. "This is not school, even if some of us are wearing schoolboy bow ties."

Game face. I was not about to let that television type get to me, even if he was disparaging my wardrobe.

"We already read the rules," I said.

"I followed the rules and forsook my bathing costume," said Chet.

"We will keep our distance from the wild monkeys," said Kitty.

"And we will not pee in the reservoir," said Pickles.

"I'm hungry!" said El Gato, even though he was obviously chewing something.

Brock picked up a megaphone. "Quiet, castaways! The most important rules were not on that list. You'll hear them now, from the most handsome rule maker on the island. Moi."

I rolled my eyes. This guy really thought he was something.

"Rule number one," said Brock. "Sometimes you'll work in teams. Sometimes in pairs. Sometimes solo.

Either way, your end goal is to win for yourself. Helping others will earn you a night in the Solitary Hut of Shame."

"That's where Mr. Puffball is going tonight!" said Pickles.

Double eye roll.

"I like your cat-titude, kitten," said Brock. "Rule number two: the camera cats can film you wherever and whenever they want. We don't care if you're crying, sleeping, or in an all-claws-bared fight with your former best friend. We will film you. Got it?"

"What if we're in the middle of a big, wet sneeze that goes everywhere and we don't have a tissue?" piped up Pickles.

Brock laughed another maniacal laugh. "Three: somewhere in the jungle is a hidden relic to be found each day, and then concealed again on the next day. It's a kind of feline totem: a wooden, cat-shaped doll with seaweed fur. The relic grants something you want, and desperately need, depending on the day it's discovered. It could be your ticket to a delicious feast, SPF 50 sunscreen, or, most important, immunity from being voted off the island."

I knew what I wanted: immunity from being voted off the island. I would find that relic, especially on Tribal Council days. Because I had to win. After *Feline Ninja Warrior*, I'd been universally adored and able to buy any ridiculous thing I wanted.

Which was exactly what I wanted.

"Rule number four," said Brock. "During Tribal Councils, one or two cats get voted off the island by your fellow castaways and sent back to the ship in the Barrel of Failure."

"That's not nice!" said Whiskers.

"I vote for Barrel of Fun instead," said Bruiser.

"Does the barrel smell weird?" said Pickles.

"Silence!" yelled Brock. "Rule number five: stay away from Mount Brock, an active and dangerous volcano. Castaways, follow my rules, or no one gets the two million dollars."

"I thought this was going to be like a vacation," said Kitty.

"With lots of hammock time," said Chet.

"And shrimp cocktail," said El Gato.

"Did somebody say vacation?" said Brock. He snapped his fingers, and a large table was carried into the Welcome Clearing, covered with platters overflowing with every kind of seafood imaginable. Even some I'd never seen before.

I'm a sea cucumber!

What a feast! This was exactly like a vacation. Now all I had to do was compete in some easy challenges and outdo my friends, and soon I'd be the new *Celebrity Castaway Island* champion.

Then I'd fill my gold limo with all the gasoline in the world and then some.

"Time for bed!" said Brock into the megaphone, even though my mouth wanted more shrimp.

He led us to our huts, which were nicer than I'd expected. Cozy, with cots, blankets, and enough thatching to keep out the elements. There was even mosquito netting and a table with a mirror and fur combs. I was to share a hut with El Gato. Looked like Brock had forgotten all about the Solitary Hut of Shame.

"Mr. Puffball!" yelled a voice. I peeked outside.

There was Brock Showman with two camera cats. "I'm here to escort you to the Solitary Hut of Shame. Follow me."

I was instructed to leave my single bag of personal items (mostly bow ties) in my hut. And off we went, past where all my "friends" would be enjoying sleep, until we reached our terrible destination:

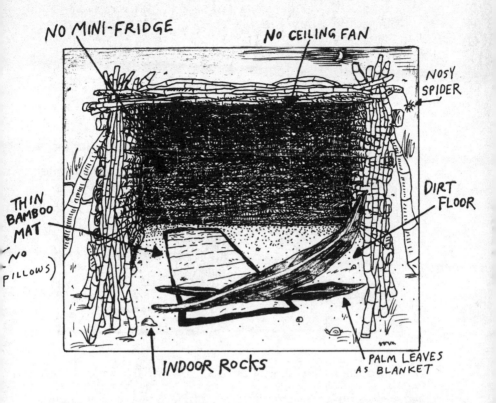

NO MINI-FRIDGE

NO CEILING FAN

NOSY SPIDER

THIN BAMBOO MAT (NO PILLOWS)

DIRT FLOOR

INDOOR ROCKS

PALM LEAVES AS BLANKET

Brock signaled to a cat who set up a camera to film my misery. "As an added bonus, the camera makes a loud clicking noise. And I'll be taking this torch with me. I hope you're not afraid of the dark, Feline Ninja Warrior." Brock and the other cat laughed, then left me alone with my sad, sad thoughts.

Chet and Whiskers were probably settling into their comfy cots right at that moment.

But could they sleep knowing I was being pun-
ished for helping them?

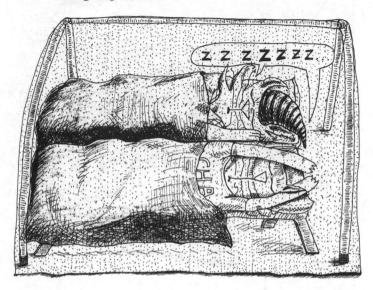

I plopped onto my thin mat (*Ouch! Rocks!*), waved
away the buzzing mosquitoes, pulled the palm leaves
over myself, and began drifting off despite the hard-
ness, coldness, and loud clicking sound.

Shelter

I have a confession to make: I never watched *Castaway Island*. I'd been too busy binge watching my *Feline Ninja Warrior* episode.

If I had, I would have known that the comfy huts my friends enjoyed were for the first night only. The rest of our time on *Castaway Island* we'd be housed in the worst kind of house imaginable.

The kind you have to make yourself.

This terrible truth was revealed early the next morning, after a rude awakening.

After rubbing sand and dead mosquitoes from my eyes, I found the gang. We were marched out to the Picnic Tables of Much Wood Rot. There, Brock raised his megaphone. "Good morning, castaways!" He snapped his fingers, and cups of milk were set before us. Then he said, "Who wants shrimp?"

Everybody wanted shrimp, of course. But what we got was less than satisfying.

"Four shrimps on my plate, too!" said Bruiser. Everybody else nodded.

"You all only have four shrimp," said Brock. "Whoever can tell me how many shrimp that makes altogether gets more."

Morning math! Very cruel indeed.

"Thirty-two!" yelled Pickles, who was promptly given a heap of shrimp.

Grrrr.

Brock laughed. It was a mean laugh. "Good job, Pickles. Remember, castaways, these mini-challenges can happen at any time."

"Thirty-two," said El Gato, in a desperate plea for more shrimp.

"I don't understand this new math," said Chet.

"Silence!" said Brock, unrolling a large scroll. And then he announced the first *big* challenge.

Choose your PARTner for today's CHALLENGE with CARE, because the two of you shall SHARE SLEEPING QUARTERS from now on.

"Pssst."

It was El Gato. He pointed to me and then back to himself, with questioning eyebrows.

I nodded. Sure, I'd be his partner. For now.

"Using whatever materials you can find," Brock said, "build a shelter. It could be a tree house. A duplex. A comfy hole in the ground. Whatever. Now, choose your partner!"

We all paired up. Me and El Gato. Chet and Whiskers. Kitty and Rosie. Bruiser and Pickles (poor Bruiser!).

Chet and Whiskers were so old, they'd probably nap the day away. Kitty and Rosie were both she-cats, and everybody knows she-cats are not good architects. Bruiser could build something amazing by himself, but with Pickles's endless chatter filling his brain, Bruiser was doomed.

It was clear who would rule this challenge. My muscles and brains combined with El Gato's need for comfort equals a sweet island home.

AH-OOOH-AHHHH!

It was the call of the conch shell. The Shelter Challenge had begun. Fortunately, I'd once read a pamphlet on how to make a basic shelter and had committed the diagram to memory:

How to Build A Basic Yurt
(to the best of my recollection)

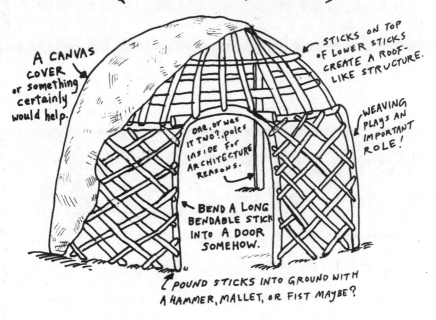

A CANVAS COVER or something certainly would help.

STICKS ON TOP OF LOWER STICKS CREATE A ROOF-LIKE STRUCTURE.

WEAVING PLAYS AN IMPORTANT ROLE!

one, or was it two?, poles inside for ARCHITECTURE REASONS.

BEND A LONG BENDABLE STICK INTO A DOOR SOMEHOW.

POUND STICKS INTO GROUND WITH A HAMMER, MALLET, OR FIST MAYBE?

First El Gato and I made a list of all the materials we'd need to build our dream home. And we called it:

LIST OF ALL THE MATERIALS WE NEED TO BUILD OUR DREAM HOME

1. Sturdy sticks to form the skeleton
2. Vines to weave together for walls
3. Palm leaves for the roof
4. Decorative seashells to spell out "Welcome" in front of the entrance

The diagram was for something basic, but with a little ingenuity, we would build something amazing.

Then came time for the Parade of Castaway Island Shelters.

"The ones with the shoddiest shelter have to share one plate of food for dinner," said Brock, pointing at me and El Gato.

The cameras all turned toward us. *Game face.* Never let them see you cry. But it was tough with El Gato next to me, acting like a kitten who had just lost his favorite ball of yarn.

"It'll be okay," I said, patting his shoulder. "Sharing isn't so bad." I forced a smile. But when it was time for dinner and we had one plate of food between us, sharing was bad.

You don't want to know.

After dinner, we were marched into the jungle to find the relic.

"What does it look like again?" asked Whiskers.

"Find it, and you'll see," said Brock.

Searching with no idea what we were searching for, in a jungle filled with densely packed trees, bugs, and pointy rocks was an impossible task. After about an hour, El Gato and I gave up and headed to our shoddy home, with our stomachs growling loudly.

We hadn't found the relic, but at least nobody else had either. It wasn't what you'd call a great day, but things could have been worse.

And then things got worse.

I FOUND THE RELIC!

Groan.

When El Gato and I finally settled into our shelter, I discovered something important: rain can and will get through a poorly built roof. It will get through all night long, whether it be misting, drizzling, or pouring.

And that night, it did a bunch of all three.

Food

El Gato and I were still damp the next morning as
we waited with the others to hear what new horror
Brock had in store for us. I was shivering so much I
missed his sarcastic greeting. But my ears perked up
when he said:

"If you want to eat, castaways, you'll have to
gather, hunt, or fish. That is today's challenge, same
partners as yesterday."

El Gato and I definitely had the advantage now.
Building a shelter was not El Gato's strong point. And
maybe she-cats, kittens, and the elderly were more
resourceful than I'd bargained for. But when it came
to finding food, El Gato was the right cat for the job.
"And now," continued Brock, "will Pickles, Finder of
the Relic, please step forward?"

Pickles strode toward Brock and proudly held out
the relic. Ugh.

Brock snapped his fingers, and two crew cats came forward with this:

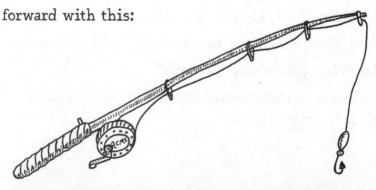

"Cool," said Pickles. "But I prefer spearfishing. And Bruiser catches fish in his giant paws. Can I give this stuff to somebody else?"

"As the Finder of the Relic," said Brock, "you may do as you wish."

"To whom shall I give the prize?" said Pickles. "It's so hard to choose."

"So hungry," I whispered.

"Look how loose my cape is," said El Gato. "I'm wasting away!"

"Pickles, remember when I made you pancakes?" said Whiskers.

We formed a circle around him. Pickles closed his eyes, pointed one paw, and turned slowly. "Eeny . . . meeny . . . miny . . ."

"Moe!" Pickles's eyes flew open. He was pointing right at Chet.

"Thanks a million, young 'un," said Chet. He and Whiskers took the pole and headed toward the beach. El Gato started after them, but I stopped him.

"We'll make our own fishing pole," I said.

We would have caught plenty of fish with my rudimentary fishing pole too. But El Gato just couldn't keep quiet.

Hunger made us delusional. The ocean started to look like a big salad bar.

"I'm going for the cottage cheese and cheddar and black olives!" yelled El Gato.

"Hard-boiled eggs!" I added.

We rushed noisily into the waves, grabbing at everything and nothing and laughing crazily.

El Gato and I left the beach empty-handed and defeated. As we dragged ourselves back to the picnic area, we passed the Producer & Crew Resort. There was a building with a sign that said "Food Shed." I stopped in my tracks. "El Gato, would it be wrong to . . ."

But he was way ahead of me.

We ate so much, so fast, hobbling back to the picnic area was not easy. When we got there, everybody else had their food set out before them.

"Look at all our fresh seafood!" said Chet and Whiskers.

"We love clams," said Kitty.

"We got them with our toes," said Rosie.

"Guava, papaya, and bananas make a lovely fruit salad!" said Pickles and Bruiser.

"Looks like somebody didn't find any food," said Brock Showman, as El Gato and I plopped down at a table.

I burped out a loud "True!"

Brock raised his eyebrows suspiciously. "Whoever wants to share their food with El Gato and Mr. Puffball may do so."

"No"—*burp*—"thanks!" I said.

"I don't think I want to share with Mr. Puffball," said Rosie.

"He's still my fwend," said Pickles.

"Let's show the boy the right way to behave," said Whiskers.

Everybody rushed over with food. We had to eat or risk discovery of our food theft. Afterward I was

so stuffed, is it any wonder I failed at the balance
challenge at Stamina Cove?

I was tired, hot, and gassy as we headed back to our shelters for a much-needed nap. But I couldn't sleep. I thought of how stinky I was doing so far: failing at house building, yoga, and finding that darn relic.

I sat up. *Does any of this truly matter?* I'd done okay without money before. Back when I was an unknown Puffball who had to take any available stunt job just to buy a slice of Hollywood pizza with one topping, pop into the occasional photo booth, and take the bus home.

The bus? Photo booths? One topping?

No way. Not after I'd tasted the salmon pudding flambé at Pacific Dining Cat. And appeared on *Opurr Winfrey*. And driven around Hollywood in my gold limo.

If I didn't win that two million dollars, I might even have to sell my bow tie collection!

My heart was racing with panic when Brock called us out again. He lined us up and said, "Now that you're all refreshed after your naps, here's your last challenge of the day. The relic is somewhere in the jungle behind you. Whoever finds it first . . ."

And then something horrible happened.

I FOUND THE RELIC AGAIN!

I let out a loud, furious hiss. The camera crew was on me in an instant. We stood on the beach, in the last rays of the blazing sun, and the heat was brutal. My tail whipped around in a frenzy.

"How do you feel about the adorable Pickles once again finding the relic?" asked one of the crew, shoving a mic at me.

Game face, Mr. Puffball! Deep breath!

I. Feel. TOTALLY. FINE.

"Ten demerit points from Mr. Puffball," said Brock Showman, "for not being honest about his feelings. Will Mr. Puffball's friends vote him off the island? We'll find out at the Tribal Council . . . in just two days."

No, they won't, I thought. Because in two days, I would find that relic. Because I had to get immunity to keep from being voted off.

My gold limo and bow tie collection depended on it.

Castaway Confessions

Hi, I'm Brock Showman! Do you know what my **favorite** part of Celebrity Castaway Island is, aside from watching celebrities **eat bugs**? It's the videotaped confessions, where each castaway reveals his or her greatest hopes and fears. **HY-STERICAL!** Here's a sampling of my favorite clips from our archives. **Enjoy!**

I hate bananas. And sand. And huts. Plus I burn easily.

WHAT AM I DOING HERE?!

BBC

Benedict Cumbercat, Episode 8

I am **not** about to quit. I've never quit anything in my **LIFE!** It's not in my **NATURE** to **QUIT!**

should I sing my song about not being a quitter now?

Mewly Cyrus, Episode 3

Chris Purr-att, Episode 8

I'm gonna do whatever it takes, hurt feelings, break bones, laugh when celebrities cry, and I'm gonna own it. BECAUSE I am in it to win it.

What was the question again?

Jennifer Pawprints, Episode 12

"We even got the monkeys on video."

We are CRAZY WILD-No joke! Some mornings I don't even brush my teeth.

We are DANGEROUS! I borrowed this shirt from BENEDICT Cumbercat... AND I NEVER RETURNED IT.

CASTAWAYS, BEWARE! We will hurt... your feelings.

BBC

CELEBRITY CASTAWAY ISLAND

Banana.

The acoustics here are AMAZING! Last night, I snuck off to Stamina Cove to sing "How Far I'll Go," and all the birds backed me up.
We have Perfect pitch.
FELI
IDOL

119

Pickles is getting on my nerves. He thinks this is The Pickles Show 24/7. If Pickles wins, I'm moving to Canada.
I LIKE CANADA!

END OF BROCK SHOWMAN PRESENTATION

Welcome to a World
of Pain

One day, Brock split us into two teams. Team Orange (me, El Gato, Kitty, and Bruiser) versus Team Gray (Rosie, Chet, Whiskers, and Pickles). Then each cat's abilities became crystal clear.

There were the Feats of Strength, when I was happy Bruiser was on our team.

There were Feats of Daring, where Pickles
had a clear advantage. That kitten was up for
anything!

Feats of Eating Bugs, which El Gato aced by a wide margin.

And Kitty surprised us all during the Feats of Endurance.

In a million different ways, with poles, puzzles, balance beams, fire, and water, with racing, digging, climbing, and spitting out mouthfuls of sand, we were challenged like we'd never been challenged before.

And the weather. Have you seen a typical weather report for a tropical desert island?

Weather Forecast/Monkey Island

SAT	SUN	MON	TUE	WED	THU	FRI
THUNDER RAIN MENACING CLOUDS	UNBEARABLE HEAT, HIGH SWEAT INDEX	30% CHANCE OF TSUNAMI	SHARK STORM	HOTTER STILL	HIGH MOSQUITO COUNT	WINDY, COCONUT DOWNPOUR LIKELY
79°F	99°F	84°F	82°F	101°F	91°F	88°F

Let's not forget the sand fleas. Sand fleas are the worst.

Through it all I had my own personal challenge: the Feat of Not Getting Irritated by Pickles.

Epic fail!

One afternoon, Brock led us to Alligator Lagoon, where eight small rafts floated, one for each of us. The camera crew was ready as usual to capture our ordeal.

"No teams for this dangerous challenge," said Brock. "Each cat works solo. Remember, these alligators will bite you in a heartbeat."

"As you see," he continued, "atop each raft sits a box. Inside each box are supplies you desperately need. You might find sunscreen and mosquito netting. Or salmon jerky and blankets. Or back scratchers and bottled water. One box has a Swiss Army knife."

Everybody started talking, until Brock raised his megaphone. "Silence, prisoners . . . I mean, castaways. Get to one box without exciting the alligators. You have five minutes, starting . . . NOW!"

The others sprang into action. I was eyeballing a box in the middle of the lagoon. Some comfy pillows were peeking out. A cat could get a good night's sleep with pillows like that.

But how to get there?

The goods were being scooped up. Rosie was almost at my box of pillows! Time to act!

Rosie jumped onto another raft, reached into the box, and yelled, "In your face, Mr. Puffball! I got the Swiss Army knife! I win!"

"Who needs a Swiss Army knife when he's got comfy pillows?" I countered. "Looks like I'm the winner here!"

We glared at each other. There was a knot between my eyebrows. And inside my stomach.

All cameras were on me and Rosie. Brock held out a microphone. "You two used to be good friends, didn't you?"

"Never!" said Rosie, glaring at me harder. Neither of us moved. It was as if we were trapped in a tangle of angry glaring we couldn't escape.

Suddenly, Rosie crouched into Kung Fu warrior stance. I mirrored her perfectly.

"Fight!" said one of the camera crew.

At that, Rosie lowered her paws and said, "I don't know who you are anymore, Mr. Puffball." Then her eyes slid away from mine. She picked up her box and left.

I grabbed my comfy pillows and left, with my head, belly, and blood all throbbing. Was I angry, sad, happy about the pillows? Or a bit of all three?

All I knew for sure was what I really wanted: to be home, back at the old MGM Studios, watching a movie and eating popcorn with my friends. One big Team Hollywood Cats.

We'd been on the island for less than a week, though it felt like an eternity. In a few hours, we'd have our first Tribal Council, when one cat from each team would be voted off by his teammates. At least Rosie couldn't vote me off. She wasn't on my team.

TEAM ORANGE	TEAM GRAY
Moi	Rosie
El Gato	Chet
Kitty	Whiskers
Bruiser	Pickles

I knew my team wouldn't vote me off the island. El Gato was my best friend! But he had recently been my enemy. Maybe he would vote me off.

Bruiser liked me. Then again, he was mad I hadn't

given him credit for being my *Feline Ninja Warrior* trainer. Maybe he would vote me off.

At least I knew Kitty still loved me, didn't she? I thought of how I'd recently fallen asleep while she was singing "The Star-Spangled Banner." That's exactly the kind of thing she does not like.

Oh no! My teammates are going to vote me off the island.

It was almost time for the Relic Hunt, which happened right before the Tribal Council. I had to find that relic and get immunity from being voted off! Once I heard that conch shell blare, indicating that the Relic Hunt was about to begin, I'd take off like a cheetah after a gazelle.

AH-OOOH-AHHHH!

Go, Mr. Puffball, go!

Bananas

Brock Showman lined us up at the edge of the jungle and raised his megaphone. We castaways eyed each other suspiciously, each thinking the same thought: *Who will find the relic?* We waited for instructions in tense silence. And then we had to wait a little longer, because Pickles and Chet had to pee.

"Welcome to the Relic Hunt," said Brock. "Today, the relic gives you a huge advantage: immunity from being voted off during tonight's Tribal Council. I'll give you a helpful hint: the monkeys have gone bananas hiding today's relic. When I say 'Go!', enter the jungle and search like your future wealth depends on it. Because it does."

Where was the hint? I didn't hear any hint. He forgot the hint! My mind was racing so fast, I almost missed it when Brock megaphoned, "And . . . go!"

I quickly came to and dashed into the jungle.

Pickles was just ahead of me. That little devil always found the relic. He rounded a pile of coconuts and veered sharply to the right, like he knew exactly where he was going.

I followed him. Pickles stopped before a big pile of bananas. Silly. This was no time for a snack. . . .

Wait a minute!

The monkeys have gone bananas. That was the hint! I leapt into action—doing a stunt cat leap over Pickles, landing on the other side, and peeling like mad. Uneaten bananas and peels piled up quickly beside us. My eyes darted around frantically. I spied a banana with something un-banana-y peeking out. Pickles saw it too. We reached out at the same time, but my paw got there first. Inside was a note.

That didn't even rhyme!

No matter. I swiveled and swiveled, searching for the X.

"Pickles," I said, "stop trying to grab the note. It's . . ." Just then I saw the X behind Pickles. I crumpled up the note and threw it as far as I could. "Go get it!"

I leapt to the X and started digging. So did Pickles. He hadn't fallen for my clever trick.

"There it is!" he said as we both spotted seaweed fur.

"MINE!" I yelled, nudging him out of the way with my shoulder while my paws reached out, grabbed the top of the relic, and wrenched it free.

Victory at last!

HISS!! Pickles was a thief! My fur stood on end and my claws were emerging when Pickles took off like a rocket. Brock's voice soon echoed everywhere. "Pickles the kitten finds the relic again! Castaways, make your way to the Tribal Council Grotto, where we shall see which two cats are the first to be voted off the island."

The torches looked especially menacing at the Tribal Council Grotto. The night had turned cold, and Brock was wearing a weird hat.

I went over and high-fived El Gato, so he'd remember who was his best buddy. Then I gave Kitty a big hug.

"Stop it, Mr. Puffball. Hugs won't save you now."

Ouch.

We castaways separated into our teams and donned our orange or gray scarves. Silence fell, punctuated by the calls of tropical birds, who were free to fly away at any time. Unlike us castaways, who were doomed to this island of total drama.

"Welcome, castaways," said Brock. "You have endured tests of extreme hardship. Some of you have been strong. Some have been brave. And some of you are losers."

Angry mutters broke out at this last word. Anger welled up in me too. How dare he call my friends losers!

"Silence!" Brock continued. "The hour has come when each team votes one of their teammates off the island. Decide now: Who shall you banish from Castaway Island?"

"The monkeys will give each of you half a coconut shell. When I point at you, vote by placing it on the condemned one's head."

Two monkeys stepped forward and handed out the coconut shells.

"Team Gray," said Brock, "will vote first. Remember that Pickles has won immunity. That means either Rosie, Chet, or Whiskers is going away tonight, back to the ship. Think very carefully before you . . ."

Brock pointed at each cat on Team Gray, one by one, until Chet had four coconut shells on his head.

"Chet is clearly devastated to be the first cat voted off the island," said Brock.

The cameras turned toward Chet. "Yippee!"

"Team Orange!" said Brock. "Who will you vote off? Kitty? Bruiser? The world-famous El Gato? Or the recent *Feline Ninja Warrior* champion, Mr. Puffball?"

My breath came fast. I started to sweat. The cameras closed in. It was almost as if the camera crew sensed I was about to be voted off.

Game face, Mr. Puffball! Brock pointed at me first.

"No hard feelings, okay, buddy?" I said as I placed the coconut on Bruiser's head.

El Gato was next. He stepped up and looked us over as if he were choosing between pizza, tacos, and seafood stew. "I need to win so my public will love me again. And I really want that money. So does Mr. Puffball. That's why . . ."

He put the coconut shell on my head! Without even a "sorry, buddy"! I turned bright red under my fur.

My best friend had betrayed me yet again! Plus the coconut shell didn't fit right.

"Exciting!" said Brock. "Bruiser has one vote. Mr. Puffball has the other. Next?" He pointed at Kitty.

"Everybody thinks I'm just an old she-cat," said Kitty. "But I didn't come here to knit. Or relax in a rocking chair. Or bake any pies. I came here to win." She held out her coconut shell. "I can beat El Gato and Mr. Puffball. They lack stamina. But Bruiser has stamina and strength. That big cat has got to go!"

YES! Bruiser now had two coconut shells on his head compared to my one. But he also had the remaining vote. He'd vote against me, of course, and we'd have a tie. Then what?

As if reading my mind, Brock said, "If there's a tie, the two losers will fight it out to see who leaves Castaway Island."

"Not fair!" I blurted. Seriously, did I stand a chance against Bruiser?

"Oh, it's fair all right," said Brock. Slowly, he raised his bamboo stick and pointed it at Bruiser.

"I came here for fun times," said Bruiser. "Island is good. But is not fun when friends are not friendly. I prefer checkers with Chet."

With that, he raised his coconut and put it on his own head.

A loud "YES" escaped my lips and victorious fist pumps escaped my paws. Everybody glared at me. "Somebody's got to go," I said.

We marched down the beach to where Chet and Bruiser would climb into the barrels and get pushed by dolphins to the Celebrity Castaway Island ship anchored just beyond the reef. I shivered as a breeze blew up the beach. Then I shivered again, because all my friends were giving me the cold shoulder.

Before climbing into the barrel, Chet put a paw on my shoulder. "Mr. Puffball," he said, "when you first came to Hollywood, you were so sweet."

My eyes welled up with nostalgia. "Thanks, old friend."

WHAM! Chet hit me with his cane. "You let fame change you. You got lean and mean, like a shark."

Something stirred inside me. Could it be remorse? Then my brain steered me back to the whole reason I came to this island: two million dollars. "Don't worry, Chet," I said. "I'll share my winnings! You'll get at least a hundred bucks."

As Bruiser pushed the dolphins aside and sped Chet and himself into the waves, my stomach felt weird. *Focus, Mr. Puffball! In it to win it!* Right?

Rosie did that thing where you point at your own eyes with two fingers and then point them at someone else—which means "I'm watching you!" And "You stink." Which equals "I'm not your girlfriend now, and I never will be."

I'd thought I'd hit rock bottom when my gold limo ran out of gas and I had only one dollar to my name. But I didn't know what rock bottom was. Until now.

Rosie's mad at you. So is Chet, Bruiser, and everybody else, too. Don't let the bed bugs bite! Good night.

Descent into
Island Madness

If you made a chart of the worst desert island problems, what would it look like?

Good chart. But you forgot something: the unre-lenting sun. Causing sweat to pour from your head to your toes, tail included. Making your throat feel like there isn't enough water in the world to quench your thirst. Burning the delicate skin under your fur and singeing the tips of your ears.

The sun. Why does it have to be so hot?

With that in mind, check out the prize for the next challenge:

The cat who shoved and yelled at his former friends, threw sand at a movie star, and lied to an adorable kitten in order to win the Maze Race at Dead Man's Cove and get that hat was ruthless. But I hope you can forgive me. My mind was twisted by one goal, which blurred the lines between good and evil:

Hanging over the next few days of sweat-inducing challenges was this question: Who would be voted off next? Then, on the ninth day since we'd first arrived on the island, it was time to find out—at the second Tribal Council.

A half hour before, El Gato dragged me back to the Food Shed.

"I'm craving canned corn," said El Gato. "Aren't you?"

"Of course," I said. "But I think Brock is getting suspicious."

Just as I'd once again broken through the lock, this happened:

We dashed off, covering our tracks as best we could, jumping into the river to throw them off our scent, and finally dragging ourselves out and collapsing on the ground.

I looked at El Gato and shook my head. "We're not doing that anymore."

"Agreed," said El Gato. "At least not until tomorrow."

Worst of all, El Gato's escapade made us miss the Relic Hunt. Meaning guess what?

At Tribal Council that night, Whiskers was voted off Team Gray. Whiskers was too nice to be a serious contender.

It was time to vote El Gato off Team Orange. His Food Shed obsession put my future in jeopardy. I convinced Kitty that she had a better chance against Team Gray with me by her side.

With two coconuts on his head, El Gato was out.

"Mr. Puffball," said Whiskers, "you used to put friends first. What happened?"

Whiskers's words echoed in my head. What had happened? And then I realized something. Everybody was trying to psych me out. I steeled my mind against their negativity. I deserved that money!

A few days later, after a meager breakfast of coconut milk and macadamia nuts, Brock led Kitty, Rosie, Pickles, and me (the only celebrities left on the island) to Suspension Cliff.

Suspension Cliff was a cruel place with a rock face rising into the sky, interspersed with ledges. Cords of twisted vine hung from spots high in the cliff down to the ground where we stood. Several monkeys were visible at an upper ledge.

"See those monkeys?" said Brock, pointing. "I've ordered them to fill a giant picnic basket with hearty food, plates, forks, and even some moist towelettes, for the first cat who gets there."

"You mean for the first team who gets there?" asked Kitty.

"No more teams!" yelled Brock. "From now on, every cat goes solo. Climb the vines, pull yourself up to a rocky ledge, climb halfway up the next vine, and then swing over to where your picnic awaits. We've applied butter to the vines to make them extra slippery."

"That's crazy," said Rosie. "Kitty can't do that."

The cameras turned on Rosie, whose whiskers were very close to Brock's. Her tail was flicking about angrily, and she emitted a low growl.

"Quitters are welcome to quit anytime they want," said Brock.

I agreed with Rosie. "Maybe you should sit this one out," I said to Kitty, touching her elbow gently.

"I'll be all right," she said, smiling bravely. "I'm tougher than I look."

AH-OOOH-AHHHH!

Pickles and Kitty ran toward the vine that would bring them closest to the picnic basket. Rosie and I hung back a moment. We wanted to give Kitty a fighting chance. Rosie looked at me with softer eyes than I'd seen in a while. Then the conch shell blew a second time.

At first, climbing the rope vine was easier than I'd expected. The butter had melted off—plus I'd built up some serious muscles over the past few weeks. We all had.

We pulled ourselves up to the first ledge, then climbed the second set of vines until we were close enough to swing over to the picnic basket. That's when I decided that if we all made it, we'd share the feast! The time felt right to show my friends I was still good old Mr. Puffball. I'd even make sure we all made it:

I wanted to give Kitty a helpful push.

But I pushed too hard.

I tried to save her, but . . .

The wrong cat became a hero that day.

Somehow we all leapt and landed safely on the ledge with the picnic basket.

"Kitty, I was trying to—" I started to explain.

"Mr. Puffball," interrupted Rosie. "You have a talent for making things worse. Let's just eat."

I sat on the edge of the cliff, sadly nibbling my salmon wrap and sipping milk from my canteen. I'd lured my friends to this island. I'd treated them like enemies. I'd put Kitty in danger. All because I wanted to ride around Hollywood in a solid-gold limo. I felt so dejected, I didn't even care about the sharp rock poking the back of my leg.

We had all the next day to find the relic that would grant us immunity from being voted off the island. I couldn't shake the urge to win and believed losing would make me feel even worse. So I woke early and searched under every rock, fern, and crab. And yet:

Back at the Tribal Council Grotto that night, my stomach was one big knot. Kitty shook her head at me. Rosie glared at me. Pickles wouldn't stop chatting. It was horrible.

And then it was time to vote.

"Sorry," I said as I voted against Kitty. "I hate seeing you in danger."

Pickles forgot where he was and put the coconut shell on his own head. Kitty voted against me. Rosie held the deciding vote. *Gulp.* Good-bye, two million dollars!

"This was always meant to be between you and me, Mr. Puffball," said Rosie. "Sorry, Kitty." She put the coconut on Kitty's head.

Rosie looked at me, and I realized I hadn't seen her smile in a long time. I have to admit, my eyes welled up. Was my dream of gold and glory going to cost me my friendship with Rosie?

We said good-bye to Kitty. Now Pickles, Rosie, and I were the last cats on the island. I slinked off to my hut, more miserable than ever, threw myself onto my pile of comfy pillows, and fell into a night of disturbing dreams.

Lost in the Jungle

arly the next morning, each of us was awoken by a monkey.

These were the monkeys who worked for Brock. Though they rarely spoke, and smelled unpleasant, they seemed harmless enough. Not like the monkeys who lived deep in the jungle, whom I'd only spied from afar.

Brock Showman was waiting for us with a mean grin. "Today is a very special day, castaways."

"Chocolate-chip pancake breakfast?" asked Pickles.

Brock laughed again. "No, Pickles. No pancakes. And no breakfast. We've prepared a backpack for each of you with one water-filled canteen, a bandanna, and very chewy trout jerky. Everybody, go to your hut and get your map and one item to help you during your final challenge. Choose wisely, for you will be all alone, deep in the jungle, surrounded by carnivorous plants, angry bugs, and poisonous berries. Then meet me on the beach for further instructions."

Back on the beach, this is what we saw:

"Can I bungee into the volcano?" asked Pickles.

"Stay away from the volcano!" said Brock, louder than necessary. "Whoever finds his or her way back to this beach first will be the winner. No more relics. No more voting. Just a race against time and danger to see who will be the next *Celebrity Castaway Island* champion and take home two million dollars. Now, what item have you chosen to help you survive in the jungle?"

Rosie's lip quivered as she stared at the proffered hat. She slowly reached for it. . . .

WHOOSH! The blades of all three helicopters started up, creating a sudden and mighty wind. The hat slipped from my grasp, flew up to the blades, and was chopped to pieces.

"That's gotta hurt!" Brock said, laughing. Never have I wanted so badly to punch somebody. "Castaways and camera cats, time to board your helicopters!" I climbed inside, and we rose into the air in a whirl of dust and noise. My camera cat came up behind me:

Was this what I'd signed up for? Hunger, blindfolds, being pushed out of a helicopter, only to stumble around the jungle for hours with this heartless camera cat filming my every humiliation?

No. I'd had enough. I took a deep breath, yanked off my blindfold, shoved the camera cat to the back of the helicopter, and . . .

WOO-HOO!

Bam! I hit the ground running, unhooked the parachute, and kept running. Yes, thorns pierced my fur. Yes, I stumbled over roots. Yes, my stomach complained that I'd jumped from a helicopter after no breakfast whatsoever. But I kept moving. That camera cat would never find me. If I was going to be lost in the deep, deep jungle, at least I'd have some privacy.

After a while, I stopped and looked around.

Where was I? I had no idea. The humid heat clung to my fur as the smell of rotting papayas filled my nostrils. Worst of all, a spider rappelled down, nearly landing on my head.

Shudder!

Man up, Mr. Puffball! I sat on a log and opened my backpack. A swig of water. A few vigorous chews of trout jerky. A bandanna secured around my head. I closed my eyes, breathed deep, and listened to the sounds of the jungle: the calling birds, wind through the leafy canopy, a river somewhere nearby. I let my breath out in a big life-affirming *whoosh.*

And, just like that, I was a new cat, ready for adventure.

"Which direction now?" I asked myself, speaking extra loud for courage. Then I remembered—the map! I found it and studied it as hard as I could. But there was no "you are here" anywhere. How could I use a map if I didn't know where I was?

"Walk until you find something familiar," I advised myself. But I didn't get far before:

So this is what quicksand **REALLY** feels like.

I struggled against the sinking sensation. Then I remembered a list I'd seen in the pamphlet "Quicksand and You."

WHAT TO DO IF YOU
STEP INTO QUICKSAND

1. Remove your backpack or other heavy objects.
2. Breathe deep for increased buoyancy.
3. Move slowly.
4. Don't panic.

That was all I remembered. I slipped off my backpack and tossed it. Not far enough—it sank into the quicksand, taking my water and food with it. *Glug, glug, glug.*

I thought of how Bruiser could pluck me out of there like he was picking a grape from fruit salad. How Chet could use his cane to pull me out. I pictured Whiskers and Kitty each grabbing one paw and yanking me out. Pickles bungee-ing me out, Rosie talking me out with her calm and soothing voice. Even if they couldn't save me, just seeing them would've been sweet.

But the truth was: I'd behaved badly, I'd hurt those who loved me, and now I was alone. Sinking into quicksand.

Yes, it was time for remorse. But, more than that, it was time to panic.

My ears pricked up. Rustling leaves. Snapping twigs. Was it just the wind, or could it be—

"I'm tempted to leave you here," said Rosie.

"I know. I've been awful."

"Yes, you have! You used to be Mr. Puffball,

kindhearted, funny, and loyal. But your desire to be famous and rich has ruined you!"

I wanted to answer but was afraid of getting quicksand in my mouth.

"Don't you have anything to say?" Rosie glared at me, then realized how close I was to extinction and leapt into action.

"Rosie, you're my hero!" I said, paws extended. "A hug of forgiveness?"

Rosie looked at my gunk-covered fur and said, "Let's wash you off in the river first."

"Looks like you ditched your camera cat too," I said as we trudged through the jungle. "Tired of having your every nose hair caught on film?"

Rosie laughed. But it was a sad laugh. "I'm tired of a lot of things. Especially of watching my old friend turn mean. I know you want that money, Mr. Puffball, but has it really been worth this stupid reality show ordeal?"

I didn't answer right away. I was thinking.

"Has it?" she asked again.

"Um . . ."

"Has it?" she repeated.

"I do like money," I said, smiling. I did not get a return smile.

Rosie crossed her paws and said, "I want a real answer."

I mentally reviewed all my actions over the past few weeks and knew what I wanted to say.

I took Rosie's paw and stared into her eyes. "No, it has not. I was a cat obsessed. But that quicksand washed the blinders from my eyes. I will make it up to you and everybody. Promise!"

"That's the best thing I've heard in a while," said Rosie, smiling. "There's the river!"

We ran and jumped in with big splashy cannon-balls.

We were having a blast until:

And that's when we knew: Pickles was in trouble.

Pickles in a Pickle

We hurried through the jungle, until we peeked through some ferns and found this:

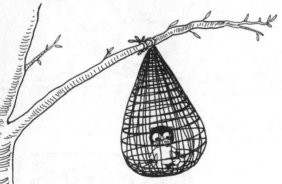

"Oh no! They're going to poke Pickles to death!" Rosie whispered into my ear.

"What can we do?" I whispered back. "There are so many of them!"

"True," said Rosie. "We're just two cats. But we have Hollywood on our side."

Rosie was right. There's a scene from a Hollywood movie to fit almost any situation. Like this one from *The Hobkit*: Bilbo's friends had been captured by giant spiders (*yikes!*) and he alone could save them. Bilbo knew that giant spiders hate to be dissed. So he leapt out in front of the oversize arachnids and lured them away with taunts like "Spiders are so dumb!" and "Hey, crazybugs!" Then he put on his ring of invisibility to really mess with their heads.

True, I did not have a powerful invisibility ring. But I did have plenty of cat-titude.

"I'll do it!" I said.

"Mr. Puffball, use my knife to free Pickles from the net while I distract the monkeys—"

"No way, Rosie," I interrupted. "I got us into this mess! I will face the wild monkeys. You rescue Pickles and get away from here as fast as you can. I will find you."

Rosie looked at me with those big eyes, and then:

Now I could do anything—even be the bait that led dozens of ferocious monkeys deep into unfamiliar jungle. I leapt into the clearing. Silence fell as each monkey face turned and stared.

"HEY," I yelled, "you silly monkeys, it's Puffball time, and I'm going to—"

I stopped. Because I saw what was at the end of the stick each monkey held: a marshmallow. In every other monkey's hand sat a chocolate-covered cracker. Pickles was lounging in the net, holding a bag of marshmallows.

"Are you making s'mores?"

One of the monkeys came toward me with a stick. And then . . .

When everybody burst out laughing, Rosie lowered her Swiss Army knife.

"Welcome to the funnest spot ever," said Pickles, popping a marshmallow into his mouth.

"I'll get you out of there," said Rosie, extending her knife toward the net.

"No need," said Pickles. "I can slip right out."

"Pickles," I said as he landed on the ground. "We heard you mewling."

"And yelling 'Bungee cord!'" said Rosie.

"True," said Pickles. "Because that tiny monkey took my bungee cord without asking."

"What happened to your camera cat?" I asked.

"Ditched him," said Pickles.

At the monkeys' invitation, we settled in around the fire to join the s'mores feast. "I don't get it," Rosie said. "I thought you monkeys were ferocious."

The monkeys all glanced at each other, their eyes shifting back and forth.

"What's really going on here?" asked Rosie.

"Should we tell them?" asked the biggest monkey. Murmurs and glances were exchanged throughout the circle—followed by lots of nodding and "yeses" and "why nots."

"That's exactly what Brock wants you to think," said the biggest monkey. "He pays us in marshmallows, graham crackers, and chocolate to do the whole 'wicked monkey' routine. It's an offer we can't refuse."

"Ours was a quiet life," said an older monkey. "We'd never even seen cats before, here on Monkey Island. Until Brock Showman and the crew landed, decided it was the perfect setting for their reality TV show, and renamed it Castaway Island. We don't like Brock or the crew, and we've often thought about chasing them off."

"We don't enjoy scaring you castaways," continued another. "But that's the gig. Just like the monkeys in *The Wizard of Oz*. They weren't evil either!"

Nobody said anything for a few long moments. Then a monkey spoke up. "I miss the days before the Hollywood cat invasion."

"It was so peaceful," said another. "Plus we roasted coconuts back then."

The biggest monkey stood and raised her hand. A silence fell. "The time has come for change. And change starts with truth telling. . . ."

"Brock . . . " gasped several monkeys.

"Forget Brock!" she continued. "I say we come clean to these nice cats. Maybe they can help us. You saw how brave they are—how willing to fight for each other." Nods of approval egged her on. "Mr. Puffball, Rosie, Pickles, we're going to tell you something we've never told anybody. It's weighing on our conscience."

"Because we have a strong code of ethics," piped up the little one.

His mom (the big one was his mom) patted his head and continued. "Every season, Brock picks a favorite castaway. And he makes us help that castaway win. This time it's Pickles. Brock says audiences love it when the kitten wins! It was our job to make sure Pickles found the relic every time. . . ."

"I thought you gave everybody hints!" said Pickles, gobbling another marshmallow. "I'm not a cheater."

"We only helped you, Pickles. And it wasn't just the relic. When we saw you getting tired, we threw you a sleeping bag, remember? And when you were hungry, we dropped bananas. We hated helping one castaway and not the others. And we're sorry."

"Thanks, monkeys, for your honesty and generosity," I said. "From where I stand, there's only one cat to blame for this situation."

"Agreed," said Rosie. "Let's ask ourselves: Who is the real enemy here?"

AH-OOOH-AHHHH!

"That's our signal to find Pickles and make sure he gets back to the beach first," said one of the monkeys.

"Do you want to get rid of Brock and his crew and reclaim this island for yourselves?" I asked.

The monkeys all nodded. Yes!

"Then we need a plan," said Rosie. "A good plan. If only we knew Brock's weakness: something we could use to really get to him."

Monkey eyes shifted back and forth. And then, as if some silent agreement had been reached, the momma monkey answered with one word:

And with that one word, we had a plan that was better than good. It was fabulous.

Volcano!

A lot happened that night.

1. We found out Bruiser had convinced the dolphins to bring all the exiled castaways to this side of the island, where he'd built a shelter big enough for everyone.

2. The gang was reunited, followed by forgiveness and reconciliation.

3. The best group hug ever.

4. Singing and dancing around the fire.

5. And the monkeys told us all about the volcano.

"One of the big reasons Brock picked this island," explained one, "is the volcano. He thought it added extra drama to the setting. He makes us call it Mount Brock."

"What did you call it before Brock arrived?" asked Rosie.

"Mr. Volcano," said the little monkey.

"Anyway," continued the first monkey. "Brock loves it as a backdrop, but he won't go near it. He's terrified of volcanoes."

"That makes no sense," I said. "Why would he pick an island with a volcano if he's terrified of vol-canoes?"

"Because Mr. Volcano, or Mount Brock, has been dormant for years. Plus Brock made us plug it with hundreds of stones. That took for-ev-er," said the big monkey.

"There's no way that volcano could blow now," another monkey said.

"Brock told us it could erupt at any moment," said Chet.

"Lies," said the littlest monkey. "That cat is always lying. Remember the big rainstorm on your first night here?"

"I sure do," I said. "El Gato and I got soaked."

"Weather machine," said the momma monkey. "Brock makes the weather whatever he wants with that terrible machine of his."

"You mean I got wet for no reason except to enter-tain Brock Showman?" asked El Gato.

"And I risked my life at Suspension Cliff even though Pickles was always going to win?" asked Kitty.

I climbed onto a big rock and waved my paws. "My good cats. Nobody should suffer the humiliations we've faced: Eating bugs. Crabs paid to bite our toes. Sleeping in handmade huts. I say *Celebrity Castaway Island* ends here. Who's with me?"

"I want our island back," said the momma monkey.

"Plus if we drive them out, we can keep the food," said another.

"We can stay at my hotel any dates," said Bruiser.

"Could I still be a two millionaire?" asked Pickles.

"Cats and monkeys," I said loudly. "Are we or are we not going to put an end to *Celebrity Castaway Island?*"

More exchanged looks, from every cat, and every monkey, and one uninvited iguana. I heard Chet say, "What's going on?"

Finally the head monkey said, "We're with you!" A giant cheer went up from the crowd. It was almost like getting an Oscar. Almost.

"What's the plan?" asked Rosie.

"In my country," said Bruiser, "all school-kittens must do volcano project. Make miniature volcano from sand, mud, newspaper shreddings, and cardboard bases. Put vinegar, and soda which is for baking—"

"We call it baking soda," chirped Pickles.

"Yes, baking soda. And grains of cherry Jell-O. Combine and . . ."

KA-BOOM! Like new tattoo? Is from squid inks.

"Eruption project in a real volcano!" said Chet. "It'll be just like that scene from my favorite old movie!"

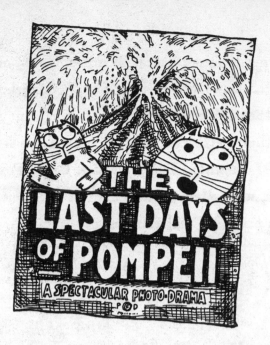

We brainstormed the details of our scheme to bring down Brock Showman and this whole phony production. And we called it:

THE MR. VOLCANO ERUPTION SCHEME

1. Gather all the baking soda, vinegar, and cherry Jell-O on the island.

2. Use drums and other noise-making devices to create volcanic-level rumbling.

3. Use flares and fireworks to create the illusion of spewing, fiery lava.

4. Keep the three camera cats from finding their way back to the beach for a long time. And steal their cameras.

We needed the cameras so Rosie, Chet, and I could pose as camera cats and film Brock's demise.

As the sun rose over the island, everybody set off on their different tasks. The monkeys led Pickles to the beach where Brock waited. Chet, Rosie, and I emerged soon after, hidden behind our cameras.

And then the real fun began.

"I've always wanted to try blowing the conch," said Pickles.

"You're a two millionaire now," said Brock. "You can do whatever you want."

AH-OOOH-AHHHH! Pickles blew that conch louder than it had ever been blown.

That was everybody's cue for: Ready, Set . . . Volcano!
It started with the rumbling.

Then the flares and fireworks went up as the volcano was transformed from "dormant" to "active."

Brock's eyes turned into giant saucers. Pickles really played it up.

Brock went screaming down the beach and leapt into one of the barrels bobbing in the surf. The real camera cats burst out of the jungle and raced to join him.

"Forget the film equipment," said Rosie, stifling a laugh. "Save yourselves!"

And the producer and crew of *Celebrity Castaway Island* floated away, never to be seen on that island again.

Escape from
Castaway Island

"**L**ooks like they're the reality show now," Rosie said, filming them floating off, scrambling aboard the ship that brought us to the island, and sailing out to sea.

"How about Brock's face when Pickles yelled 'Magma'?" asked Chet. "Did you get that?"

"Oh, I got it," said Rosie.

"We did it!" yelled Pickles, throwing the conch shell into the air. We all cheered and waved happily as the *Castaway Island* ship sped away from us.

"I just want to say . . . ," I said, watching the ship recede into the distance. But I forgot what I wanted to say. Because as my eyes watched the ship (our only way off the island) get smaller and smaller, I realized our excellent plan had a giant hole in it.

Sure, we were on a beautiful tropical island. Yes, we were all friends again. True, there were enough marshmallows to last a lifetime.

But how could I ever become a famous movie star this many miles away from Hollywood? A sob was just escaping my lips when:

Bruiser. He really is the best.

We loaded up the ship with coconuts, canned goods, and drinking water, and pushed it down the beach and into the surf. There we found more new friends:

We had some great footage. We'd saved the day. We had our way home. Now it was time to say good-bye to Celebrity Castaway Island, or I should say Monkey Island, and sail back to Hollywood.

"Good-bye, monkeys!" I said. They waved and smiled. But some had the kind of smile that only goes up on one side. Rosie whispered something in my ear, and I nodded. "Would any of you monkeys want to come with? We'd be happy to introduce you to the Hollywood monkeys we know. Most of them are scriptwriters."

Some of the monkeys wanted to stay and enjoy having their island back again. Or at least, their island to share with all the other animals who lived there.

All we had to do now was enjoy the voyage home, taking turns at the helm, with Bruiser providing our daily catch of seafood and Pickles manning the crow's nest.

> HAS ANYBODY SEEN MY BUNGEE CORD?!

> WHEE!

It was smooth sailing, except for one difficult moment. It happened one afternoon when El Gato said to me, "We had quite an adventure, Mr. Puffball."

I laughed and said, "And it all started because you lied to me about a volcanic eruption in downtown Hollywood."

"True," said El Gato, laughing and slapping his knee. "Did you really believe that?"

El Gato let out a big sigh, leaned against the railing, and stared out to sea. "Mr. Puffball, I've been a superstar for a long time."

"So?"

"So I used to constantly get asked to star in all the big movies, no audition necessary. But not anymore. Now I have to seek out parts. So when Victoria Bossypaws asked me to audition for a big part in a major motion picture on the same night I was supposed to go on *Celebrity Birthday Cake Wars*, I couldn't say no. I had to go! And I was embarrassed to tell you that I, the great El Gato, had to audition like a regular actor."

I leaned on the railing next to El Gato. "What major motion picture?"

He looked sideways at me with his eyes squinting against the sun. "I can't tell you."

Just then Bruiser rang the lunch bell he'd made out of coconut and seashells. El Gato started toward the picnic deck, but I put out a paw to stop him. "From now on, we tell each other the truth. Because that's what friends do. Okay?"

"No more lying, I promise," he said, pulling me into an unexpected hug. Sweet!

As we strolled over to lunch, I guessed which movie he had auditioned for.

"Was it *Paw Trek?* A new *Furlock Holmes?* A remake of *Hairy Pawter?*"

"I can't tell you until we get back to Hollywood and I meet with Victoria Bossypaws."

When we landed at that dock in the Port of Los Angeles, dozens of journalists and paparazzi were waiting for us. Evidently, Brock had leaked a crazy story about some kind of celebrity mutiny, and they were all eager to question us. Rosie decided this media attention was just the thing to create some buzz about the *Celebrity Castaway Island* movie she was making.

It felt great to be home with my friends. After lots of napping and eating, everybody got busy with different projects.

Whiskers and Kitty stole the show in *Prancing with the Stars.*

El Gato and I helped Bruiser and Pickles make a commercial for the Body Shop for Tough Cat Training. The boxing kangaroo was in it, too. He was a good actor with a charming Australian accent.

Rosie and Chet spent many hours at MGM Studios, editing the footage from our *Celebrity Castaway Island* adventure.

Then one day, Rosie gathered everybody together in the screening room. "Friends, our time on *Celebrity Castaway Island* had everything: extreme weather, death-defying adventures, surprising twists, and an awesome revenge plan." She winked at me.

I blushed bright red under my fur. But it was a happy blush.

"Thanks to all your contributions, *Escape from Castaway Island: The Reality behind Reality Television* is a movie we can all be proud of. This documentary reveals the truth about our experiences. And now, enjoy!"

After Whiskers and Kitty brought in giant bowls of popcorn, the lights went down and:

Eight innocent cats made their way to Castaway Island, unaware of the grueling ordeals that awaited.

There, they were subjected to unimaginable
humiliations, such as being forced to eat bugs.

The cats were pitted against each other until all
semblance of friendship and compassion had
vanished.

Monkeys were portrayed as vicious and unpleasant,
when in fact they are totally awesome!

A fake volcano eruption sent Brock Showman and crew into exile. The monkeys were free, and our heroes escaped the horror that was . . . Castaway Island.

The gang and some monkeys sailed home,
happy in the knowledge that good had once
again triumphed over evil.

And that was it—our reality TV adventure, as told by
a fabulous up-and-coming director: my friend Rosie.
(And a plug from the monkeys.)

Oscar Night

As you may or may not know, one of my all-time biggest dreams has always been:

The Oscars are awards given by the movie industry for a variety of categories: Best Actor, Best Actress, Best Movie, Best Costume Design, and many others, including Best Documentary.

Have you ever seen a documentary? A documentary is a movie about something totally real, such as:

March of the Penguins is a documentary about a community of emperor penguins (real penguins, not actors) who huddle, waddle, and belly slide their way around Antarctica. Amazing!

Imagine how excited I was when Rosie showed me
this letter she got about our documentary:

THE ACADEMY of MOTION PICTURE
ARTS and WISDOM (AMPAW)
525 Starstruck Lane
Hollywood, CA 90028

Rosie Pringle and Chester P. Grumpus III
MGM STUDIOS
3200 Hollywood Street
Hollywood, CA 90046

Dear Ms. Pringle and Mr. Grumpus,
Congratulations! The Academy
has nominated Escape from Castaway Island:
The Reality behind Reality TV for an Oscar.
CATEGORY: BEST DOCUMENTARY
WHO IS INVITED TO OSCAR NIGHT:
The directors and the entire cast
(Except Brock Showman. He's awful.)
WHERE: The Dolby Theatre, Hollywood, CA
WHEN: This Sunday

Sincerely,
The Academy

"Winning an Oscar would be a dream come true,"
said Rosie.

"Ditto times a thousand," I said.

"Just being nominated is such an honor," said Kitty.

"I once won an Oscar," said Chet. "I wonder where it is."

Soon it was time for the big event. The gang and I piled into the van I bought after selling my gold limo, and off we went to see if we would win an Oscar. Oh, the celebrities we met! And the fancy candies we enjoyed! And the cushy seats! It was a magical night, even if we hadn't won an Oscar.

But, reader, we did win.

We all jumped up, patting each other on the back, cheering, and giggling like kittens who had just been given a whole basket of yarn. As we made our way over to the stage to accept our Oscar, I thought of all I'd been through in the past few years.

I thought of all the adventures and misadventures that are so well recounted in my other two books. So much had happened.

And here I was at last, about to accept my first Oscar.

Smile, Mr. Puffball!

Fortunately, we all had a chance to give a short acceptance speech.

Actually I had more to say. But the "time to get off the stage" music came on, so I stopped talking. Plus they turned off my mic.

The after-party was amazing. My favorite part was like a scene from a movie. Remember at the end of *Cutie and the Beast*, after the Beast figures out he shouldn't be so beastly and turns back to a handsome prince, and then Cutie and he dance together? Well . . .

A week later, I found out what movie El Gato had auditioned for, back when he tricked me into going on *Celebrity Birthday Cake Wars*, which, come to think of it, wasn't really such a bad experience.

The best part was, it looked like I was back on the road to becoming a movie star. El Gato had talked Victoria Bossypaws into casting me in *Guardcats of the Galaxy Vol. 2* after all.

Wow! I'd just won an Oscar. I was back with my friends. I was going to be in a major motion picture with El Gato and Chris Purr-att. I used the rest of my gold-limo money to buy Chet that vacuum cleaner he wanted. In other words, life was awesome.

Not bad for a kitten from New Jersey with nothing but a big dream.

COMING SOON TO A
THEATER NEAR YOU!

The True History of
CASTAWAY ISLAND

We monkeys founded this Island LONG AGO.

We found it right in the middle of the ocean. Like it was waiting for us.

SO... MONKEY Island.

Marshmallow.

Grandpa says it's always been Lizard Island. And he's SO OLD. He's older than my mother.

Yep.

ACTUALLY, It's Parrot Island. Say it. Parrot Island. Again. Parrot Island. GOOD.

We wild Boars think of it as more of an ISLET. BOAR ISLET.

It's been Mosquito Island since before I was born. And I was born 9 days ago.

BLOOPER REEL

THE UNCOOPERATIVE SHARK

REVENGE OF THE BUG

THE UNEXPECTED COCONUTS

KUNG FU SCENE GONE WRONG

THE OVERRIPE BANANA

WARDROBE MALFUNCTION

Any similarity to actual cats, living or dead, is purely coincidental . . . or is it?

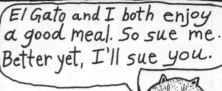

I'm a sharp-dressed reality **TV** producer, just like Brock Showman. You call that a coincidence?

El Gato and I both enjoy a good meal. So sue me. Better yet, I'll sue _you._

I like naps. Chet likes naps. I play checkers. Chet plays checkers. Plus the author has known me since I was a young 'un. She stole my life!

I'm a kitten. Pickles is a kitten. Also, where am I?

Celebrity Castaway Island Corporation
A Division of Reality Adventures, Inc.
175 Scratchpost Lane
Hollywood, CA 90069

Pickles
MGM Studios
3200 Hollywood Mews
Hollywood, CA 90046

Dearest Pickles,

We have good news, and we have bad news.

The good news: per our contract, as the first cat to make it back to the beach *on Celebrity Castaway Island*, you have won $2,000,000. Congratulations!

The bad news: when Brock Showman said "dollars," he really meant "samoleans," the currency of Monkey Island (formerly Celebrity Castaway Island). In today's market, the exchange rate for the samolean as compared to the US dollar is as follows: 400,000 samoleans = 1 US dollar.

If you choose to return to Monkey Island, your samoleans will get you approximately 1,000 coconuts. Or about 12,000 marshmallows.

If you choose to go to your local bank and trade your samoleans for cash, you will receive $5 American.

Again, congratulations on being the final winner ever of *Celebrity Castaway Island*, a show which has been canceled until such a time as we can strike a deal with the resident monkeys.

Sincerely,

Swifty McMillions

Swifty McMillions
Chief Financial Officer
P.S. Please do not sue us.

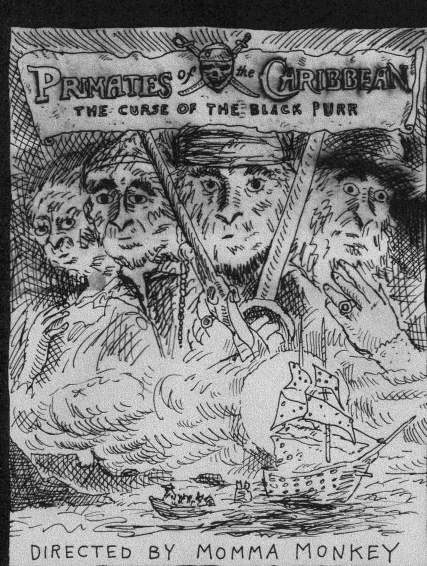

Acknowledgments

I am grateful to my readers, and especially those who reached out to me with emails, letters, and drawings. You are what it's all about! Thank you to Andrea Jacobsen for sharing your impressive knowledge of reality shows, and thanks to all my Secret Gardeners for ideas, encouragement, and lots of laughter. Laura Boffa, I greatly enjoyed our shared drawing events and will always remember the dancing pickle and will miss you at Games Night. Thanks, Nancy Inteli, for being a fellow cat person and for your love of Mr. Puffball. So much appreciation to my friend and the world's coolest editor, Jill Davis, for pushing me to be the best I can be. Luana Horry, thanks for your thoughtful feedback! To Amy Ryan, Katie Fitch, Carla Weise—you are a joy to work with, and you make my books look absolutely fabulous! Bethany Reis, thank you for correcting Mr. Puffball's grammar and making him look smart. Megan Barlog and Ro Romanello, thanks for keeping Mr. Puffball in the celebrity loop! Thanks to everybody at HarperCollins—copyeditors, designers, marketing, publicity, and sales people—your hard work is truly appreciated! To Lori Nowicki for all your kidlit knowledge, brainstorming help, and everything else! To Malaprops Bookstore and especially Amy Cherrix for eternal support of my books. Also to Firestorm Books, Bank Street Bookstore, and all independent booksellers for creating wonderful spaces for book nerds. Thanks to Sal and to my sister Rita for bringing Mr. Puffball to your schools! To #bookvoyage, #booktrek people, and teachers and librarians everywhere for spreading the love of reading. Linda Marie Barrett, I look forward to our future writing retreats and book tours! To Madeline for first envisioning the fantastic idea of Mr. Puffball on a desert island. And to my husband, Hank Bones, for sticking by me even when I'm running madly around the house yelling, "Deadline! Deadline!"

CONSTANCE LOMBARDO

would love to be swept away to a beautiful desert island except for the:

1. Tropical bugs
2. Tropical heat
3. Quicksand (I watched a video about it. Scary!)
4. Having to wrestle monkeys for my fair share of the coconut milk

So she lives instead in Asheville, which is nothing like a desert island, but is a lot like a beautiful town in western North Carolina, with her husband and daughter. Her two cats, Gandalf the Grey and Myrtle, also live there, and one of them is very happy to eat all the bugs he can find (G.G.).

If she did live on a desert island, her desert island foods would be:

1. Carrot cake
2. Lasagna
3. Avocado toast

Her desert island books would be:

1. A sketch book (and watercolor set!)
2. Ursula K. Le Guin's Earthsea trilogy
3. *The Complete Idiot's Guide to Escaping from a Desert Island*

She is thrilled about the two other Mr. Puffball books:

1. *Mr. Puffball: Stunt Cat to the Stars*
2. *Mr. Puffball: Stunt Cat Across America*

Writing and illustrating books is her dream come true.